She's the Prey, He's the Stalker

Jackie Adams

Deer Run Press
Cushing, Maine

Copyright © 2022 Jackie Adams

All rights reserved. No part this book may be reproduced or transmitted
in any form or by any means, electronic or mechanical, including photo-
copying, recording, or by any information storage and retrieval system,
without written permission from the copyright owner.

This is a work of fiction. Names, characters, places and incidents either
are the product of the author's imagination or are used fictitiously, and any
resemblance to any actual persons (living or dead), events, or locales is
entirely coincidental.

Library of Congress Card Number: 2022932378

ISBN: 978-1-937869-14-4

First Printing, 2022

Cover photo by Ben Pierce.

Published by
Deer Run Press
8 Cushing Road
Cushing, ME 04563

Chapter 1

Bursts of flashing light come filtering in through the tiny slits of the vented window. It's almost as if the lightning is bringing itself inside of this madhouse. I'm not sure how much longer I can hide before he finds me. The thunder is roaring with the same intense fury I want to be screaming with. My heart is thudding out of my chest. I remind myself to remain calm and to stay quiet. I swallow down hard and hold my breath.

"Cassie, I can hear you." His repulsive voice echoes throughout the empty attic. "When I find you, there won't be any need for words. You will FEEL the frustration you have caused me."

I know he means business. I had smelled what I can only assume was a dead body that was rotting away in the basement. The stomach-turning stench greeted me like a nightmare from hell. My only prayer is that it is not my boyfriend, Jeremy. Suddenly, I feel the back of my head explode in a million different directions.

By the time my eyes open, he's dragging me by my ponytail. My fingernails are dredging through the wet, muddy grass. I'm camouflaged in the earth's soil, and every part of my body feels like it's sinking with his long, harsh pulls. I try to reach up, but I can only move my eyes. I quickly shut them again. Maybe he'll think I'm dead. Maybe he'll just drop my body off somewhere and leave me be. It could be hopeful thinking, but that's all I have left. Please, please, I think to myself, leave me alive.

It's a few months earlier. Life is perfect. I may not have realized it before, but I acknowledge it now. I have the dream home, complete with a white picket fence. I have a loving boyfriend who takes a caring interest in me. We have three dogs. Every time I come home, they greet me like I'm the best thing that's ever happened to them.

"Cassie, when is the spaghetti going to be done, babe? I'm starving." Jeremy comes into the kitchen and kisses the back of my neck. His hands follow my figure.

"Keep that up, and it won't get done!" I'm stirring the sauce and hold out a spoon for him to try some. "How does it taste?"

"Mmmm, more." He sticks his finger into the pot. I wiggle my eyebrows up and down.

I take out the noodles and put them on a plate, "Hey now, no finger dipping."

He pulls the cheesy garlic bread from the oven. "This smells great. I can't wait to dig in."

"You and me both. What do you want to drink?"

"You set the table, and I'll grab a couple of Mountain Dews. Sound good?" He looks over the counter at me with that gorgeous smile of his. God, what this man does to me! Everything from his brown, curly lochs to his full, luscious lips. And his eyes... his puppy dog eyes. One look at those and I'm putty in his hands.

All three dogs come running in. They're hoping for some table scraps. They keep a fair amount of distance to let us eat in peace. We never give them food while we're eating. It'll just cause them to beg without a moment of rest, and who wants that?!

Over dinner, Jeremy asks, "Do you have clients scheduled for today?" I'm a real estate broker. I met Jeremiah, an architect, while he was designing a house on some property I had sold.

"Yes, I have three clients, actually. Right now, business

is booming. I just might get my she shed after all." I've been wanting a cozy escape to a paradise in my backyard. I imagine relaxing inside it and reading a book when it's too hot outside to enjoy the hammock. I could possibly make it my own personal office at home.

"I could design you one and have it built in no time at all. I don't see why you're making such a big deal of it." He takes another bite of his spaghetti.

I raise my shoulders up a little higher in defense, "I want to do this myself, Jeremy. It means a lot to me. I don't care if you design it, but I'm going to pay for it." I breathe in the positivity and release a deep breath for any negativity regarding the possibility of not selling a house.

"I have to go." I give him a quick kiss on the cheek and make my way out the door. As I'm making my exit, I yell, "Sorry for leaving you with the mess. I'll get it next time."

The drive to the estate was a short one. It's only a few subdivisions away from my own. The house is in superb condition. I enter the house and set a bouquet of springy day flowers on the island before the prospective buyers arrive. It's a personal touch I like to add. It makes the house feel more like a home.

I hear a knock. I open the door and smile, "Come in!" The Casings heads are going in every direction as they look at all the handcrafted molding throughout their surroundings. "And in here, you will see plenty of open space." I guide them to the kitchen and living room, which is one spacious area.

It's an hour later, and they're already putting in their bid. I'm going to miss this house. Due to the estate's enormous size, it was on the market for over a year. It looks like it has finally met its match. I happily take the papers and put them in a folder. I let them know, "I'll get your bid in right away. I think you put in a wise one. I'm sure they'll take it."

I'm on my way to a second house. Out of nowhere, an eighties station wagon rolls right into my lane! After I honk the horn frantically, it guides back into its own lane at the very last second. My phone rings, "Cassie Jennings."

"This is Marge. The Landlocks called me. They're wondering if their appointment is still scheduled for later this afternoon?" Marge is my superior. She owns our company.

"That's strange, I wonder why they didn't call my cell phone. I gave them my business card."

Marge takes what sounds like an aggravated breath, "Well, either way you need to call them. How'd the appointment go with the Casings?"

"They just put in a bid." I'm anxious to get to my next client. "Right now, I'm on my way to visit with the Smith family for the Shepard Hill Subdivision cottage. I have a feeling they're going to love this place. If not, I'll introduce them to a few other places I have in mind."

"Alright," she sucks in another breath. "I'm proud of you, Cassie." It comes out muffled, as if she's choking on her own words just trying to say something nice to me.

I click the phone to end our conversation and pull into the parking lot. It has a three-car garage. I'd say it's only two, but I guess you can squeeze a third one in. Although, it would be a very tight fit. I get out and see the cottage was just power washed. It's looking spectacular. The Smiths pull in behind me. I can see their smiles broaden as they take in the two-story stoned retreat.

"Mr. and Mrs. Smith," I extend my hand out. "It's a pleasure to put a face to the voice."

It's a few hours later, and they're fully satisfied with everything they've seen. It's not our first house. In fact, we've seen over a dozen of them. They let me know they'll discuss it together over dinner and call me. As for me, I'm in a hurry to get to the rustic, log cabin on ten acres. I don't want to be late for the Landlocks, especially after they called my boss to confirm it.

I get an eerie feeling as I drive under the arched tree limbs that lead to the next sure-shot home. It's like a scene from a horror flick, where the car breaks down and someone spooky jumps out of the woods. I guess I'm just too much of a city girl. Upon arrival, the log cabin is breathtaking. I see the Landlocks have already arrived. They're looking at the garden in the front yard. I meet and greet them and take them inside for a tour.

We go through the two-story high foyer. "This is quite the welcome entrance," Mrs. Smith remarks. "It's quite exquisite for being a cabin." The previous owner still has it decorated with his and her furniture. Mrs. Smith is right. It's not what I imagined from the outside.

"I'll be here in the kitchen if you need me." I take a seat at the wrap around breakfast bar that overlooks the dining and living rooms. As Mr. and Mrs. Smith wander around the cabin, I check my phone to see if the Casings bid was accepted. So far, nothing. I do, however, have a text from Jeremy.

Jeremy: I'm missing you already.

I can hear Mr. Smith talking from the library room upstairs, "The asking price is fairly low for what we're getting. I guess it's the commute of the ten-mile range to the nearest city. Since we're retiring, I say we don't play around. Let's give them the asking price."

I can also hear Mrs. Smith's reply, "Really, you mean it, honey?! I'd love to retire here. It's perfect for us."

They walk down the stairs and turn toward the kitchen, "We will take it! Asking price and all!"

Mrs. Smith asks, "Would they be willing to sell some furniture?"

I smile and feel my eyes gleam with eagerness, as I think to myself, she shed here I come. Then I answer, "I don't know I'll have to ask the owners." After Mr. and Mrs. Smith leave, I text Jeremy back.

Me: Guess who has two bids in?

Jeremy: Two?! You're amazing, but I think you already knew. I guess I better start designing your she shed.

By the time I get home, I'm feeling exhausted. I'm not

even sure why. It's not like I did any paperwork yet. I see Jeremy isn't home. I go into our bedroom and pull off my heels. I grab my cell phone and laptop and carry them both into bed with me. It's only six o'clock, but it feels more like ten. I text:

Me: Can you bring home some Chinese food?

Then, I check my voice text to see if there have been any missed calls. None! Zilch! Feeling disappointed, I go to my laptop and bring up the paperwork so I can get a head start on filing. I have a good feeling that both bids will be accepted. If not tonight, then it will be tomorrow.

A good hour goes by, and I hear Jeremy opening the door. I yell, "I'm in the bedroom." The closer I hear his footsteps, the more I smell the Chinese. I say, "You sure know the way to a woman's heart."

He smiles and puts the bags on the bed. He responds, "That's not the only way." He leans in for a kiss.

<h1 align="center">Chapter 2</h1>

I wake up and hear the rain against the windows. I snuggle in closer, facing Jeremy. As I'm taking in his closed eyes, I wonder if it's me he's dreaming about or if he sees nothing more than darkness. I don't have anywhere to be today, so I take in the pleasure of falling back to sleep. I turn, as he wraps his arms tighter around me.

An hour passes, and I wake up to the smell of bacon. I look around and spot Jeremy's white shirt. I slip on some panties and button his shirt around me. As I enter the kitchen, I smile and think of Hank, "Hey, good lookin'! Whatcha got cookin'?"

He smiles back at me. "Well Good afternoon, sleepy head. My interview was cancelled due to the rain, so I decided to make you a gourmet omelet." He uses the spatula to flip it with a zing.

"Thank you, honey." I grab my cell phone off the counter and check the voice mail. I smile, in no surprise I have four messages waiting. As I listen, I have two bids accepted. A few seconds later, the Smith family want to continue looking. They felt the stone cottage wasn't big enough for their family. They reminded me they have two children not even in their teens yet to think about. I say, "Honey, you'll have to excuse me. I need to call The Casings and Landlocks to let them know their bids have been accepted."

He yells, "Woohoo! Two for the babe!"

I make my way back to the bedroom and open my laptop. I fill out some more of the paperwork while the phone is ring-

7

ing. I get comfortable. I let both families know their bids have been accepted. It's my favorite part of the job, making people happy with their dream homes. Today it's been two, so I'm doubly happy! I fill out the rest of the paperwork when Jeremy walks in.

He lies beside me and says, "Baby, you work so hard. Are you ready for breakfast?!"

I give him a kiss then reply, "I sure am, handsome. Let's do it!"

He pinches my tit and I laugh. I follow him into the kitchen where he already has our breakfast on the table. He also has some papers sitting next to my plate and juice. "What's this?" I ask.

He leans in over my shoulder, "Those are the rough drafts of your she shed." He kisses the back of my head.

I take a bite of bacon and look through the sketches with the blueprints of it. I get to the third one. I say, "This is it babe! I love this one." It has a big spacious area and a private bathroom. It's perfect for what I need! I tell him, "I decided to make this into my office. I'm tired of doing my work off my bed, and using your office just feels cramped to me. I feel like I'm invading your space."

He takes a drink of his coffee, "That's fine, hun. I know my office is a bit male for your taste, but you're never cramping my style. However, I do understand your need for privacy and space." He takes in a fork of his eggs. He says, "I liked the third one too. So, you want all glass windows from ceiling to floor then?"

"Yes, that way I can see out to the garden. And your location in the yard is divine! It gives me the exact amount of tranquility that I need." We live on two acres with well water. The well has been a recurring issue we've had to maintain, but I figure the scenery is "well" worth it.

After breakfast, I do up the dishes and find myself back in the bedroom on my laptop looking up more houses for the Smith family. The market during spring is kind of limited because the kids started back to school. Most are situated for the time being. I keep looking, though. I find a few I think are big enough and I print out their resources.

I get up and get dressed. No need for a shower, it's my grunge day. I put on a hoodie and grab some of the balls to play fetch with the dogs. "Come on boys, let's go outside and play!" We go inside the fenced area. There's plenty of space for them to run. I throw out two balls, and one stays behind with me watching in awe as the other two run. "Don't worry boy, you're still just a pup. You'll catch on soon enough."

Bandit and Scamp bring back the ball, and of course, the pup, Columbo Columbus, starts to tackle them trying to retrieve it. They're such good boys! Even together they do fine. I'm proud of each of them.

After about an hour of playing in the backyard, I decide to go in and see what my boyfriend is doing. I find him in his office. "I'm still working on the she shed," he says.

Now it's my turn to look over his shoulder, "It looks good, babe." I give him a kiss on his cheek. "Do you want to take a break and snuggle on the couch to watch some Netflix with me?"

"Ah, I'm in a moment, though. You pick the movie, and I'll finish up here." He sorts through some screenshots.

Half an hour later, he meets me at the couch. "Did you find anything good?" He brings me my favorite, a margarita. He sits on the couch next to me and gets under the covers too.

"What's the special occasion?" I ask.

"Two sales in one day's pretty special! We're celebrating." He takes a drink of his rum.

"Thanks for recognizing, toots." I give him a wink. Then I take a sip, and I show him a movie I think he'll like. As I start to push play, my phone rings.

"Hello, Jennings."

"Hi! This is Mrs. Smith. I was just wondering if it were possible, could you show me the two houses today? My husband has to work through this week, and we're making find-ing a home a priority. Our lease is almost up, and we're run-ning out of time."

I say more to Jeremy than to Mrs. Smith, "Oh, you need me to show them to you today?"

I have a concerned look on my face. Jeremy gives me the go-ahead nod. "Okay sure, can you give me a few hours? I need to make some phone calls and get ready. I'm not used to working on Sundays."

Sure enough, a few hours later and I'm showered and ready. Yet, I'm full of regret. I was enjoying a snuggle with my man, and I only ended up with a sip of my margarita. I'm fully aware of how great and understanding my boyfriend is, but I'm disappointed he didn't give more of an argument to be with me. What was he supposed to do, though!

"I'm leaving, babe. I'll be back later." I give him a kiss and head out the door.

Shortly after, I'm viewing another subdivision house called the Craftsman. It's beautiful. It's definitely large enough for their family, if not too big. I turn the lock, and before we know it, we're inside looking right into the hall. To the left is a sitting room with a fireplace, and to the right is a living room. As we walk further down the hall, we walk past a full bathroom with a shower, a master bedroom, and into a huge kitchen. "Do you think this is more to your lik-ing?"

They both smile, and then Mr. Smith says, "We'll look upstairs."

"Okay, I'll meet you in the living room."

I already know what's upstairs. There's a craft room to the left, and if they walk further down the hall, they will be met by three more bedrooms. They're not just standard bed-rooms either. They have loads of storage, and each bedroom is huge. There's none of the regular stuff-yourself-into-a-bedroom theme.

As they're looking through the rooms, I text Jeremy:

Me: Sorry.

Soon after, the Smiths are back downstairs. Mr. Smith says, "This is it! You did it, Miss Jennings. You found our dream home."

Mrs. Smith wraps her arm around her husband. "I love this place. We decided we will make a bid."

I want to jump up with glee. This makes three sales in one week. That's more than I've had in months. Yet, I remain cool. "Okay, what would you like to bid?"

We talk about business together. They decide on $220,000. The asking price is $240,000. "I think you have a good price. That's what I would recommend."

I show them out, and then walk to my Prius. "Honey, they want the house!" Of course, I had to tell Jeremy. I was too excited not to call him. "I finally found one they like."

He says, "That's great, love! Sounds like it's time for a baby."

I choke on his words, "A baby?" That was a quick and sudden change of topic. "Don't you think we should get married first?"

He laughs, "I thought you'd never ask." I laugh with him.

"I'll only marry you on one condition, though. It has to be a small wedding. Maybe even at a courthouse. Or we can go to Vegas?"

I respond, "I don't think this is the time or place to discuss this." I cough, eluding anything else that I might have to say.

He says, "Okay, okay. To the back burner it goes, but I'm not letting you get off so easily on this topic again."

"Love you."

"I love you too." He responds. "Oh, make sure to get home fast. Your margarita is waiting for you, and the Netflix choice is mine since you left."

I laugh, "On my way now, cuddle bug."

Chapter 3

She's better than I expected. If only my wife wasn't here, I could bedazzle her. The way she talked to me on the phone, I could tell she wants me. Her soft voice has changed into a more business dynamic tone now that the wife is present. Look at the way she walks and leans into me. I must make another appointment where it's only the two of us.

Who would have known finding a house for the unthankful wife would have led me to my dream gal. All I have to do is play my cards right. I wanted to shove her against the wall and kiss her like no man has ever kissed her before. If only she knew how badly I wanted her. Hopefully, she's not distracted by my wife. I hope she wasn't influenced by her at all.

Later that afternoon, I walk down Sanford Street. I'm trying to recollect my thoughts, but I'm consumed by her. Maybe I should give her a quick call so I can hear her voice again and see if anything has changed since she saw my wife. It's not easy being a married man to an ungrateful woman. All she does is want and need. She never lets up either. She's always questioning me about my where abouts. She's constantly telling me what needs done around the house. She never makes me feel good enough. This is her fault, really.

I walk in and the wife greets me. "It's about time you got back. Dinner is almost ready."

"Alright. I'll be in my office," I make my way through the hall before she has time to say anything else. Three kids-turned-to-teens later and the woman thinks she owns me. The wife makes me feel like a boy, but my dream gal makes me feel like a man.

Possibly later this evening I can drive past her house and get a glimpse of her through the window. I'm not really a peeping tom, though. I'm a curious man with needs. I want to be closer to her. What's her taste in style? I want to know more about her. This way, when she admits that she can't stop thinking about me, I'll be prepared to know what kind of woman I'm getting involved with.

I hold her business card in my hand. It has a logo of a house outline printed in blue. It has too much information on it. It gives her address, cellular, and home phone number. Doesn't she know how dangerous that can be?! She needs a strong man like me to protect her. Yes, I'm who she's missing in her life. There's enough of me to go around.

By the time six o'clock rolls around, I'm passing by her house. Her lights are on, and there's a car pulling into her lot. She comes outside and greets a man. She gives him a kiss. What the hell?! Who's that? She's already cheating on me?

I've been following her since I met her. She has a usual spot at the coffee brewery she attends every morning. I think I'll go tomorrow and strike up a conversation with her. Once she sees me, she will forget about the other man. I'll remind her of what we felt this morning with the eye contact we had.

Once I get back home, I enter my office and open my laptop. I study her Facebook page. I print up her picture and fold it, putting it into my wallet. Yeah, I'm going to make her mine. I don't see any mention of the man I saw in her parking lot. I wonder who he is. It states she's single on her profile. Er, maybe he's new. Either way, I better make my move tomorrow.

I feel so turned on, as I lie next to the wife. I start kissing her, but she pushes me away complaining how tired she is from the cooking and housework. All she does is stay home all day. How's that so hard? She should try working six out of seven days a week and see how she likes that! The wife pushing me away is only pulling me closer toward my dream gal.

By the time I wake up, I'm almost late to meet her. I hurry out of bed, take a quick shower, and pick out a nice suit. I'll charm her, as she has me. I pick out my special blue tie. The color matches her business card.

The wife says, "I made you some breakfast." God, she sounds like my mother. The way she's been so cold and distant, she may as well be.

"I'm not hungry, and I'm running late. Thanks anyways." I'd give her a kiss, but I can tell she's dreading it. Er, I skip over it. She doesn't appreciate me the way I need to be. The way I want to be. I grab my brief case and leave.

I'm pulling alongside the curb when I see her. She's with the man. They're entering the coffee brewery. Why? How am I supposed to chat with her now? Something needs to be done about this. If I go in, I can get a better look. I can eavesdrop on their conversation. It will make it easier to find out who he is.

I park and slam my car door a little harder than I meant to. I rush inside, so I'm not too far behind them. Just then, a woman turns around in a hurry and spills her coffee on my white shirt. My tie is drenched. She says, "I'm so sorry, Mister."

I hold my hand up, stopping her from touching the stain, "It's okay." I turn back around and head toward my car. I get in and stay waiting for them to come back out. I get my camera ready on my phone, so I can take a few quick photographs.

I'm starting to feel impatient, but then I see them finally leaving. She's smiling as he is talking. She looks happy, but I can make her happier. He's just a skinny thing. He looks rather young too. He doesn't have the skill and appreciation I do. I'd give her someone to hold. I snap a few pictures.

I decide to follow them to see where they're going next. We turn down a few side streets, and then get on the interstate. We go to Baskin Park. They park at the History Museum. It looks to me like they're sightseeing. I've had enough of them for one day and decide he's not right for her. I am. I make my way back home.

Chapter 4

"Can you believe it, Jeremy?! Three houses are signed on now. Each confirmed and notarized. I can get a desk and a chair." I'm over ecstatic, as I ramble on about the furniture I'm going to buy for my she shed.

He's sitting there holding out my margarita. "And finally, some time to ourselves." He smiles at me, as he hands me my drink.

I gladly accept it and take a sip. Then I say, "It feels so good to do this for myself. You're always doing everything, and it makes me feel bad." I'm sitting on the couch and tap the seat next to me. "Move over here by me."

He gets up and sits next to me, "With all that excitement I didn't want to get too close with your hands flailing about." We laugh.

"There's really not much more for me to personally do tomorrow. How about we skip a day of work and go to the museum?" I ask.

He tilts his head and looks lost in thought. "Hmm, which one? The Art or History?"

I put my margarita on the coffee table, "How about both?" I scoot in closer to him. "I'll wear that short skirt you like so much with my suede boots."

"Oh, no fair. Now I'm in." He playfully says.

I lay my head on his lap and before I know it, I'm waking up. He must have covered me while I was sleeping. He obviously exchanged himself with a pillow. I make my way to the bedroom. "Where are the dogs?"

He answers, as he straightens his world map tie, "I let them outside, so they wouldn't disturb you this morning." He turns to look at me, "Are you still wanting to go to the museums?"

I smile, "You bet I am!" I hurry to the closet and grab my skirt and boots.

We feed the dogs and leave for the ten-minute journey. Jeremy is driving. He pulls out of the garage and asks me, "Do you want to stop for a coffee?"

"Sure!" I loosen my seatbelt some. I feel squeezed in. I roll the window down to get some fresh air. I watch as we pass by some wooded areas with beautiful trees. They're not bare anymore. Their leaves are getting full. I notice some Tulips and Lilies budding. "It's such a beautiful drive to town."

Jeremy turns on the radio and switches through the stations and says, "It's nice only being seven miles from it too." We start singing together.

Once we arrive, Jeremy opens my door like the stud he is. "Coffee madam?" We go inside, and the place is packed. Shoulder to shoulder people! That surprises me for a Monday.

I tell Jeremy, "It's nice to have a day off, but this is starting to feel like work."

He leans in closer to me, so he doesn't have to yell. "Best coffee in town."

After we get our drinks, we go back to the Prius. We decide we will go to the History Museum first. Jeremy loves it there. I think he could get lost in it for hours reading every detail of the exhibits. During this time, the History Museum is exploring Beyond the Ballot. It's about woman's suffrage and events leading up to the passage of the 19th Amendment in 1920. I'm pretty psyched up for this!

He takes my hand in his, as he uses the other to drive. "Are you hungry?"

"Um, not yet really." I shift my sitting position to be more comfortable. "How about we eat at the Art Museum when we go there? They have both the restaurant and café." He pulls in and parks. From there we enter the big, spacious building with an airplane hanging from the roof and polished floors that shine its reflection.

A few hours pass, and I look toward Jeremy. "Okay, now I'm starving."

He looks over at me, "Me too. Ready?"

I answer, "Ready Freddy!"

The Art Museum is in the same park and probably an acre away. Right now, they have an exhibit of Javanese Batik Textiles. I'm not sure what it's all about, but I'm going to find out. First though, I'm going to eat! Just then my stomach growls. Jeremy says, "I heard that from here."

I smile at him. "Let's go to the restaurant where we can relax and take in the view of the park."

He nods, "Sounds good to me!" As we walk in, he says, "Let's have a steak to celebrate you getting your closings."

"This day just keeps getting better." I give him a hug before we sit. We practically have the whole restaurant to ourselves. There's one older couple sitting catty-corner from us. I stare over at them, and then back at Jeremy. "I want to grow old together like them."

He sets his menu down, "Are you saying you're not old now? I was thinking of trading you in for a nineteen-year-old."

I hit him with my menu, "That's not even funny. Especially these days."

An hour goes by, and we finish eating. I'm excited to get downstairs and see the exhibit. I have no idea what it's about or even what it is. I feel ignorant, but if I already knew it would be a bore. Jeremy tells me he's going to see the Van Gogh. He always loved his story of fighting dragons and cutting his ear off. I tell him, "I'll meet you in the front lobby in an hour?"

He grabs me in for a hug and kiss, "Sounds good to me."

As I start walking, I look back at him, "You sure say that a lot."

He calls back, "I'm savvy that way."

I text him:

Me: Oh, you mean you're savvy by telling me everything sounds good so you can be agreeable all the time?

I smile, as I put the phone back in my pocket. I'm looking around and find the exhibit. I grab a pair of ear buds, and as I take a tour it audibly guides me through what's taking process and how it works. It's interesting how they use wax on cloth. A lot of the displays are used in ceremonies such as dances and plays.

Before I know it, an hour is up. I hurry to the front entrance when I realize Jeremy isn't here yet. I text him:

Me: I'm going to the gift shop. Meet me there.

I go to a bookshelf of artists and all their works they created within their timeline. I look at the jewelry. I get excited when I see the clothes. I see some Batiks they have on display. Nice! I roam over to the handmade wallets and think of getting Jeremy one as a surprise. I feel a hand on my shoulder from behind me and realize it's Jeremy. I turn around and say, "You're late."

"Yeah, I met a man that was as interested in Van Gogh as I was. We talked the whole time. He works for an insurance company. He gave me his number. Looks like I made a new friend. How was the exhibit, babe?"

I put the wallet back and tell him, "I loved it. I learned a lot, but I didn't make any friends like you did."

We hold hands as we walk out of the museum. "Are you as tired as I am?"

"I say we go home, snuggle in bed, and watch movies the rest of the night."

"Sounds like a plan to me!"

Chapter 5

The night flew by, and we both crashed by ten. I'm searching through the closet. "Honey, do you remember the purse I bought at Michael Lynn's?"

He slips on his white t-shirt to go under his blue button up. "Yeah, what about it?"

"I've searched this whole room and closet. I can't find it." A few boxes from the top shelf fall on me. Luckily for me, they were lightweight.

Jeremy comes running up to me. "Are you okay?" After he sees I am, he laughs. "You look a mess!" Then he says, "Did you accidentally put it in the box you are going to take to Good Will? You might want to check it. It's in the garage on the top shelf to the left. Though, I'm not sure I can trust you with boxes right now. If you want, we can both go outside and search it."

I sigh, "No, that's okay." I give a bit of a pout. "I don't want you to go out of your way. I know you have interviews today."

"That I do! Big ones too. Did I show you the rough draft of the cedar home I designed? I have three different views. I really think they're going to go for it. It'll cost them a pretty penny, though!"

I let out a squeal, "I'm so excited for you, honey!" I feel a slight sadness come over me, and he prepares to leave. "I'm going to miss you. We've spent so much time together the past few days. This is going to feel off."

"Yeah, I get it." He straightens his tie. "You'll be fine, though. Don't you have to meet your clients today at the bank?"

I huff, "Only two. The third one is tomorrow." I take in a breath. "What I need are more clients."

He responds, "Stingy."

"No, no. I like to stay busy. Busy as you."

He leans into the mirror, checking out his facial features, "Honey, I'll be home about the same time you will."

"What? A woman can't miss you?"

He pinches my butt, "Not just any woman. My woman!" He then gives me a kiss on the cheek, grabs his keys, and leaves.

"Here boys!" I take them to the yard and play some fetch with them before getting ready for the bank appointments. I actually have two lined up. Should be easy cheesy! I throw the ball again, and then look over to the area my she shed will be, right behind the hammock.

After about thirty minutes, I leave the dogs outside. It's not a cold morning. No rain, all sunshiny. Perfect for them to have some time to play before they get locked inside the house. I grab a cup of coffee and bring it to the bedroom with me. I take a few sips and set it down. Then, I jump in the shower, brush my teeth, and find appropriate attire. A black suit with a silky, white blouse. I look around for my purse again. It matches my heels. No such luck! I'll go in the garage when I get home, after I make dinner. Disappointed, I manage to stroll out of the house without the dogs jumping on me and leaving muddy paw prints all over my blazer. Though it's sunshiny today, the night before last it rained. The ground hasn't had time to dry yet.

I make a few calls, making sure everything is set at the bank, and sure enough it is. This is good news! I look at my smart watch, a few things are going right this afternoon. Besides, it's not like I can't replace the purse. It's just that I really needed it. It is the same brand as my heels.

A few hours later everything is signed, sealed, and delivered. They got their keys and I got my check. I'm on my way home when I realize I need to stop at the grocery store and get a few things to cook tonight. I decide on fried tacos, just like my mom taught me to make them. Speaking of, I need to call her soon and check up to see how her and Dad are doing. It's been a while since we've had a talk. I get so busy. Then of course, there's also Jeremy's parents. I know, I should plan a dinner and invite all four! I'll find out when Jeremy isn't busy.

By the time I get home, Jeremy is already there. "Hey, babe!" I put the bags on the counter. "I bought taco makings for tonight."

He comes over and gives me a kiss, "Sounds good. I have great news!"

I want to say, so you got the job, but I bite my tongue. "Oh?"

"Yeah, they took my design. They actually loved it. You should see it, Cas! It's beautiful. The house sits by a creek. It's twenty-two acres. It's mostly treed. It's breathtaking. I feel so at peace there."

I walk up to him and wrap my arms around his waist. "I'm so proud of you, Babe." Then, I start taking the ingredients out of the bags. "Hey, that reminds me, what do you think of me setting up a dinner date for our parents? It's been a while."

"Oh no! The four of them together?! Nah, I'm just kidding. Sounds like fun to me." He takes out the pan to fry the beef in. "Have you talked with them about it yet? Mine might be out of town. They're rarely home since they've retired. They're always traveling and flying off somewhere."

"I know what you mean. My parents bought an RV, and I rarely hear from them ever since. I think they have more of a life than we do."

"You know, we're both doing really good right now. I think it would be nice to buy a cozy cabin somewhere to the west of us. One with a lake and a pool."

I let out a huge breath, "Honey, you know winter is com-ing. My sales drop to an all-time low."

"I make enough to cover us. Why can't I do this for us? It's either the cabin or a baby."

"We don't have enough room here for a baby. My she shed, remember? Otherwise, I'd turned the spare room into an office."

His voice gets really excited, "We can sell this place. I can design our own home. How about that? You'll even have your own private office."

"Do you really want me to become dependent on you? Because that's exactly what will happen, Jeremy. I don't trust many with a baby while it's young. I won't be able to work."

"So, take some time off! You said winter is your down time anyway. Come on, Cas! We've been talking about the right time for a baby. It's been three years."

"Okay, if I stop my birth control. It's only going to be AFTER the home is built and lived in. Deal?!"

He laughs, "So, we're doing deal or no deal regarding a baby?! We can't make this a proposition. But yeah, I'm in. That way we can adjust to living there. Sounds perfect to me!"

I look at him and say, "I always wondered what it would be like to have us both in one child. Would he or she have your eyes, your curls? Your full lips? My chin? My nose? I don't know, but I'm willing to find out. In fact, the more I talk about it the more I want this. I want us. What if we have the house built, and we have our wedding there?"

He takes me in his arms, "Sounds like a dream to me. Let's do it!"

He gets down on one knee, "Will you marry me, Cassie Jennings?"

"I sure will, Jeremy Banks. Hmm," I pull him up, "Jeremy and Cassie Banks. It has a ring to it if I must say so myself."

"Speaking of rings, I think this Saturday we should go pick one out. What do you think?"

I copy his famous line, "I think it sounds good."

We kiss, and for a moment life stands still and I realize... I'm going to get married!

<h1 style="text-align:center">Chapter 6</h1>

"Damn broad. I can't believe she was with him again! Doesn't she ever get tired of running around on me?" I study her in one of the photos I took. Then I take scissors and cut him out of the picture. I go upstairs and look through our albums trying to find a photo of me that would fit good next to my woman.

That's when the old lady walks in. "What are you doing?"

I put the album down on the coffee table, "I was strolling through memory lane." The nasty bat sits next to me. I wish she would get out of my hair. She's been bugging me all day long. This is exactly why I like working six out of the seven days. Normally, I'd be working today, but my dreadful boss called and said he didn't need me.

She picks up the album, and starts ranting about everything we did, when, and where. As if I'm too stupid to remember. I take the album from her. "Did you make lunch?"

She says, "Yeah, I was thinking how's tuna salad sound?"

"Great," Then I think to myself, now leave me alone woman. Reluctantly, she does. I get back to browsing the photographs. Aha! I found one where I would be facing my dream gal. This is perfect! I put the album back on the shelf.

I go back in my office and take a seat at my desk. As I do, I bang my knee on the metal of it. "Ouch."

She calls in, "Everything okay in there?"

"Er, fine, everything's fine!" I rub my knee, and then I look at the photo. I look around my desk for tape and find some. I put the two of us together. All I need now is a frame. I can take it to work and put it on my desk there. I wonder what she's doing for dinner. It wouldn't hurt to drive past her house again. Maybe I can get a glimpse of what she's wearing and how she has her hair! Is it up or down? I bet she's missing me.

I quickly eat my tuna salad while the wife is babbling on about her day. I think she's never going to shut up then there's finally silence. Oh, thank God! All she does is criticize or complain anyway. Tuning her out is one of my best traits. I've seen her face so many times. I'm sick of her. I probably know every expression she's giving without even looking. We've been married twenty-five years. We tolerate one another.

"I have to go out. I'll be back later." I grab my keys, and I make sure I have the photo with me. "I'll see you tonight." My full intention is going past her house and getting a look at her. Hopefully, she's outside, or I'll have to drive by later tonight. Her lights will be on. I'll see her inside. Maybe I should send her some flowers anonymously. Or I could buy her a gift and leave it at her door or car. She should feel as special as she is to me.

I drive past her house, but I don't see her outside. I park my car down the road and decide to sit there a bit. I'm waiting to see if she comes out. She could be in her backyard. I get out of my car and decide a nice, little walk wouldn't hurt me. I have on my jeans, so it's not like I'm in my suit. I walk past and decide to take a hike through the tree line. Yes, as I suspected, she's in her backyard. I think she's playing with a dog. Oh, that's certainly a dog, a big one too.

I hike my way back to the street and walk to my car. Her hair is in a ponytail. She has on a hoodie and a pair of jeans just like I do. A match! It comes as no surprise to me, though. She's my gal! I wonder what kind of present she would want. During my drive home, I debate it. On second thought, I don't really want to be at the house with the wife.

I stop at a bookstore instead. I park under a tree, so my car can have shade. It's nicer that way, really. Er, I see the man that was with her go inside. I wonder if it's a good idea if I do too. I could make nice with him. Then again, he might see me. I'm not sure it's the right time for that.

I've already eaten, so going out to lunch is a no-go. I guess I'll go to the lumber company and get the cement blocks the wife was asking for. It will complete the backyard patio. She's been on me about that for two months. Maybe it will keep her out of my hair. I could up and leave the raggedy old thing. I mean, I've seen so much better. Why should I be stuck with her? Then again, the kids would be traumatized. Why would I want to leave them with her?

I go inside the lumber company and get a tow cart. I make my way to their gardening section and find the matching cement blocks. I put in one, two.... until I've reached ten. My back starts hurting then. I know it's enough, for now at least. I won't be able to tell for sure until I get home. By the time I'm finished, it's dark outside.

I drive past her house again. There she is. I park across the street. I can see her sitting on her recliner and reading a book. I wonder what she's reading. Did the man bring that to her? I should have gifted her a book, but he hogged the scenario. Such a jerk! I shouldn't get too worked up. I could be wrong. Maybe it's a book she already had. Er, maybe not.

I go inside, and right away she asks, "Where have you been? And don't tell me work. I already called there."

"Geez, woman! I went to the lumber yard and got the cement blocks for the patio." She's pacing back and forth in the living room. It's making me feel her nervous energy.

"Really?!" She seems happy. She gives me a hug, and I close my eyes, imagining it's my dream gal.

I say, "Hug me tighter."

Chapter 7

It's already been a long day, and Jeremiah still isn't home. I take the three dogs out to the backyard and play with them. "Come on Columbo Columbus you can keep up with them!" He really tries, and you know what, he succeeds. He goes out further than the other two and collects the ball in his mouth. He doesn't bring it back, though. Instead, he runs past me, expecting me to run after him. Ah, he wants to play chase. I let the other two dogs run after him, instead. Columbo Columbus is a bloodhound. Bandit is a goldendoodle, and Scamp is a West Highland white terrier. Scamp is my eldest. He's fourteen years old.

By the time I get in, I'm exhausted. I take a quick shower and put some grey sweats on. I add to it one of Jeremy's t-shirts. I throw my hair up in a bun and go into the kitchen to see if we have anything to make for dinner. Nothing! I text Jeremy:

Me: Can you bring home some pizza?

I go into the living room, but I'm not really in the mood for TV. Instead, I browse through the books in the bookcase. I find one. It's called, "Your Timing Is All Wrong." I'm curious if it's a suspense, so I read a quick brief. I decide without Jeremy home it's not the book I want to read. Too spooky! I ponder through a few others. Finally, I find "The Book Note." Looks good!

I curl up on the couch and start reading it. I hear a noise outside. I'm a little spooked after reading the other book, but I get up and close my blinds. I go into the kitchen and make me some hot cocoa. Then, I cozy back into the book. I hear my phone ding.

Jeremy: Sure thing, hun. You want taco or supreme?

I put my book on my lap and pick up my cellular.

Me: I want both.

I have an Android, but Jeremy has an iPhone. We always argue over who has the best. Of course, he thinks he's always right. He's high tech, so he likes having everything updated all the time. If they come out with a new phone, he has to have it. Same with his iPad and apple watch. It's his money, so I don't complain. Anyway, he's always using them for work.

After reading for about an hour, I start getting restless. I'd take the dog for a walk, but all three would want to come. There's no way I can walk three dogs at once. They're just not trained for that. I put the book down on the end table next to the recliner.

I go into the bedroom and open my laptop. I start looking at land for sale. We'd want something on a hill. He wants a river or creek, and we definitely want a beautiful view. I spend thirty minutes browsing through listings. I hear the front door open. "Jeremy, babe, is that you?!"

He says, in a playful sarcastic tone, "No. It's the pizza delivery man. I'm here to please you in any way I can."

I come walking into the kitchen. "I've been browsing listings of land. Do you have anywhere particular in mind?"

He sets the pizza down on the counter, "Well, actually, I do. I was thinking along the same creek the cedar home I'm designing is on. What do you think? I could take you to see it tomorrow?" He gets a paper plate, grabs a slice of pizza, and hands it to me.

"Are you sure you wouldn't rather be on the river? You can fish, boat, and have a lot more water that way." I take a bite of taco pizza.

He grabs a supreme for himself. "Actually, I thought we could have both. Where the creek runs into the river. What do you think?”

I take a bite, and with a mouthful I say, “I want something on a hill.”

He smiles at me for talking with my mouth crammed. “You’re going to love this property! Would you like to see it tomorrow? The front is on a hill, but the back is flat. When we have our child, we can fence it in and have a playground. We can even have a pool if you want.”

I walk to the refrigerator and pull out a 7UP, “Wow, yes, I want to see it! What time?”

“How about after we sleep in late? It’s not like we have to be on a schedule right now. We’ll be close to my job, so we can take both our cars. I can head straight over to the cedar property right after.” He carries his second slice of supreme pizza over to the couch.

“I’d also like to see the cedar property. It’s pretty obvious it’s what has inspired you.” I sit on the couch next to him. I’m excited and nervous at the same time. I know Jeremy, and when he becomes involved in something he makes it happen fast. I can see myself being pregnant. I think that’ll be the easy part. Birth terrifies me. Me, a mom? One thing is for sure, Jeremy will be the best dad ever! Even in worst case scenario, if he ever left me, God forbid, I know he’d be a good father.

“Hey, what are you sitting over there thinking about?” He nudges me with his arm.

I swirl the top of the 7UP can with my finger, “I’m thinking about being a mom. How excitingly terrifying it makes me.”

He kisses me on the forehead, “Babe, you’re going to be a wonderful mother. We need this in our life. I’m surprised you’re not more focused on the wedding.”

“I can’t, until I see the land and the design of the house. I mean, it can be anything. I do know I want a summer wedding with lots of flowers, sundresses, and sandals. The wedding will be fun. I’m not nervous about that. It’s the motherhood that terrifies me. I know I'll be a good mom, but there's so much I don't know about it. My brother and I have a huge age gap, so by the time he was born I was busy in my own life. I know nothing about babies."

He laughs, "Your eyes are huge. Stop focusing so much on it. When you become pregnant, we will find some classes. I'll buy you a ton of baby books. We can even subscribe to a parenting magazine. We'll both learn as we go. We can do this. Not to change the subject, but when are we having dinner with our families?"

"I've arranged it for Sunday. Both will be in town, though your parents may be a bit jet lagged." I put my finger on my chin, "I wonder what I should make."

"Fried chicken and mashed potatoes." He crosses his legs. "We haven't had that in a while."

"Chicken and potatoes, it is!" I flip through the channels. "I'm not sure I'm going to be able to stay awake much longer." I yawn, "Babe, are you getting tired?"

"I'll race you in there!" He jumps from the couch and sprints toward the bedroom door.

"No fair. I have to clean up this mess and put the pizza in the fridge." I squash my 7UP can and put it into the recycling bin.

Shortly after, I'm in the bed and snuggling next to Jeremy. As he plays with my hair, he says, "You know, becoming a father is scary too. Not so much in the younger years, but in the teens... I worry. I know the two of us together can get through it, though. Imagine a little one coming in here, Mom... Dad... can I lay by you?"

"I think about holidays too. How much fun they will be! Taking our child to see Santa. Finding cute, little Halloween costumes." I pinch his nose, "I guess we both kind of skipped out on the diaper changing part."

He says, "Positive things only."

Chapter 8

"I don't know about you, but I slept good last night." I walk behind Jeremy and wrap my arms around him. "Did you already eat?"

He takes my hands and pulls them tighter around his waist. "Yes, I just ate a bowl of cereal. Something light on my stomach."

I tuck in the tag on the back of his shirt, "What are you doing in here?" I look at his spacious office. We put in a loveseat about three months ago.

"I'm going over the designs. I don't have to be at the job site all the time, but they want me to routinely check in to oversee it. I guess they don't want the workers messing it up."

I go inside and slip on a nice pair of blue jeans, a spring blouse, hiking boots, and grab my denim jacket. I walk back into his office where he's putting all the papers inside a folder. "You're going to show me the cedar place today, right?"

"I certainly am, but I think you'll like our future landscaping much better." He looks up from his folder and winks at me. "By the way, I don't have to stay there this morning. I can just check on the place, while we're there. We can just take my car."

I go into the living room to sit on the couch, so I can put on my hiking boots. I yell back to him, "Is casual wear okay?"

"Yes, babe. I know I'm dressed to the tee, but next time I'll wear jeans. It's a mess there right now with us excavating the ground." He clears his throat, "But this time I wanted to wear a suit, in case the owners, the Stephens, are there."

As we're walking out the door, I ask him, "How far is it from here?"

"It is about 25 miles. Eight miles from town. It takes us longer to get there because it's on the other side of the town." He unlocks the car.

I'm so excited! Last night, I fell asleep imagining how it must look. All kinds of sceneries are going through my head. I put on my seat belt and get comfortable preparing myself for the scenic drive. "Do you want to tell our parents that we're looking at land to build our house on? Or do you want to keep it to ourselves for now?"

As he drives, he says, "No, we can tell them. I'd wait to mention the marriage and baby for now. We don't want to hit them with everything at once."

I mention, "I'm going to be sad not living by the covered bridge anymore."

He says, "Babe, where we are going, you'll forget all about it. You'll see beauty out of every window. It won't just be trees like we have now."

"Uh, I love those trees." I row my window down, staring out.

As we pass through town, I ask him, "Can we go through a drive-thru, so I can get a coffee?"

He answers, "Music to my ears."

By the time we get there, I'm already halfway done with my coffee. I'm feeling anxious. We drive down a narrow black top street that has two sides covered with a variety of trees. Jeremy explains, "I'll give you a heads up. It's a gated community. It takes an electronic card to get inside."

"That actually makes me feel safer, though with three dogs I wasn't worried." I let out a nervous laugh.

We enter through the gate and drive a few hundred feet, when I notice a small community center. As we drive through further, I see a tennis court, basketball court, and a children's playground with a playhouse. "How cute!" I could imagine bringing my child there and reading while he or she plays on the slide.

We go up a hill, and there's a swimming hole. It has two slides. One for little children, and it appears one for bigger children and adults. In the center, it has a fountain that keeps the water moving. I notice how blue the water is. We drive further, and I see a river. He drives up a gravel hill and stops. "This is it, Babe. This is the spot I want to build on."

He comes to my door and opens it, reaching his hand out. I grab it, and he leads me to the left. We walk a bit then he says, "This! This right here is the view we would have from the front windows. This is where I want to build our cottage house. What do you think?"

I stand in awe, "It's breathtaking, Honey. I couldn't have found a better place. This is perfect, and it's on a hill just like I wanted!" I wrap my arms around him, and we both silently stare in awe. After, I turn and look at what would be the backyard. We don't really need a swimming pool or playground. It will be perfect for our three dogs to run around in. Maybe we could put a hot tub and a BBQ patio back there. I have all these ideas running through my head.

He pinches my butt, "Are you ready to see the cedar estate I'm working on?"

"Sure." We make our way back to the car. "You know, we're going to need four-wheel drives for the winters."

He nods, "We will take care of it. One thing at a time. We will get there, and it will be so worth it!"

He stops at the cedar place. "This is it," he says.

I open my car door, walk to the front of it, and sit on the hood. "Wow, this is beautiful too." The house has already been started, so I can get a glimpse of the future the family will have here. I see a three-story cedar and log cabin. "It's huge," I remark. There's a creek that runs downhill alongside of it. I say in a real low voice, "You're right, I like our property better, but this is gorgeous! I'm getting so excited,

Jeremy. I want it right now."

"Me too, Babe, me too." He walks up to the green, wooden door. "Do you want to see how it's coming along on the inside?"

"Yes, I'd love to." I follow him around, as he gives me a tour. Each window has its own landscaping view. I see what he means when he says our windows will have a better view than the property we are on now.

When we're finished, he takes me to the side. "What do you think of the property I showed you? Do you agree it will make good land for our home?"

I'm practically jumping up and down, "Yes, yes, yes! I'm completely happy with it."

He grabs my earlobe, "Should we buy it?"

"Yes, I already wish the house was built." We both laugh.

"Designing it is the fun part. You'll help me every step of the way. Then, when it starts coming together before your very eyes, it's a rewarding feeling. You'll experience it soon enough."

"Can we go look at the property one more time before we leave for home?"

He gives me a broad smile, with his eyes gleaming, "We sure can."

The ride is all blacktop, until you get to the driveway of our future property. As I said before, it's gravel. I guess putting blacktop on such a high hill wouldn't be a good ideal. When we pull in I hurry to get out. I walk to where our front porch will be. "See where the hill declines? I want a rock garden there with a gravel pit. We can use park pebble in it. It'll be a good spot for our child to play in the yard. We can have ivy surrounding it. I also want floor to ceiling windows... should we do picture windows instead?" I have so many questions and thoughts running through my mind.

"Easy, slow down. The garden area is a must do. Brilliant idea! Since you're not getting your floor to ceiling windows in your she shed, sure, we can put them in there.

What kind of exterior do you want? Stone, brick, log…"

I interrupt him before he even finishes, "Stone!!! Stone and cedar!!!! I like the mixture of both."

"We'll have to be careful living out here with cedar. We will need to keep a close eye out for termites."

"I'm going to make my office a library/desk room. Oh my God, I'm so excited!!!" When you're looking down, there's just enough room for a porch. The hill in the yard will be a rock garden. Then it flattens out, which is where I'll put the gravel pit. I'll add a bonfire station there. Then, it goes into a grassy yard. In front of the grassy yard is a black top road. Then, it goes into a grassy hill that leads down to the river. Jeremy loves to fish, so I know this is a dream come true for him. I climb down both hills. I take a seat in front of the river.

Jeremy joins me, "It makes you never want to leave, right? That's how I felt when I started designing the cedar estate. I knew I had to show you this place."

I stand up. I have a handful of semi-flat rocks. I start skipping them across the water. "I will probably have nightmares about our child getting out and drowning."

"We'll put a lock on the top of the door. You'll never have to worry about such a thing. He or she can have swimming lessons while young. It'll work out, you'll see." He starts walking back up the hills, and I follow him.

As we get inside the car, I look over the roof of it and say, "I really love this place, Jeremy."

The drive home wasn't bad. There's so much to think about. If we had a wedding at the house, where would we put the dogs? Will three dogs get along fine with the baby? All kinds of questions that have me worried.

He looks over at me and then back at the road, "You're awfully quiet."

I run my fingers through my hair, "I have a lot to think about."

Chapter 9

I'm outside. I'm setting the cement blocks the way the nag asked me to. I go inside and grab the radio. I put it out back, and I turn on country western music. Er, Johnny Cash... I turn it up. I go back to laying the blocks. A few minutes in, and the wife comes out. She says, "I thought you might like some lemonade."

"Yes, put it on the picnic table. I'll get to it when I'm done putting down three more." I should have said yes mommy, but I didn't want to stir up an argument. Laying these isn't as hard as I thought it would be. I'm getting older, and my back restrains me from doing a lot of tasks I'd like to do.

I wipe the sweat from my forehead and take a big gulp of the lemonade. She better be thankful after this. Maybe I'll even get me some. I walk back over and start laying the rest of the cement blocks.

A few hours pass, and I'm finished. The backyard looks different than before. It looks a lot better. I go inside and wash my hands. "I'm going to hop in the shower."

When I'm finished getting dressed, I decide it's time to check in on my dream gal. I wonder what she's wearing today. I bet she's thinking about me. It's too bad the wife decided against moving into a new house. At the same time, good riddance of her! Now that she's out of the picture I can spend some quality time with my girl.

As I'm getting in the car, the wife stops me. "Where are you going?"

"To the store. Stop asking me questions, woman." I roll

the window up, while she's still standing there and continuing to go on and on about me leaving. I can't hear her, but I can see her lips moving.

The day has turned into dusk. I pass by her house, and she's standing at the window looking out. She looks to be waiting for someone. I wonder if it's that guy again. She seems to be getting serious with him. I'm going to have to make my move before they become serious. Er, maybe a gift is too much in the beginning. I guess I'll go home and think up a plan. Maybe home isn't the best idea! I could go to the library or Barnes & Noble. Barnes & Noble would be the best option. I don't think they close until ten. I can buy a tablet, make up a list, and work on a plan.

When I arrive at Barnes & Noble, it's pretty quiet. A few people are wandering through the store, but none at the coffee shop table area. I purchase a pen and a small journal-type tablet. This will work!

I order a decaf coffee and sit at a corner table. She should be sitting here with me. Yes, I know she'd enjoy it. I should have stopped and asked her when I drove past.

I start my list:

1. Meet her acquaintance and start dating her.
2. Meet up purposely to her knowledge by accident.
3. Buy her a gift and leave it on her car.
4. Send flowers anonymously.

I look it over, and I like number one. Maybe then I can find out who the man is she's been spending so much time with. Tomorrow, I'll bump into her best friend. It's easy to know who she is. She used to be at her house continuously. One day I followed her, and she went to a new job. So, as of lately, she's been too busy to visit.

I look at my watch and notice it's 9 pm. I better go home, before the wife has another proverbial fit. I put my tab in the bag and the pen in my pocket. I grab my keys and head out the door.

I crawl in bed next to my wife and shut my eyes. By the time I open them, it feels like I've only slept for five minutes. Yet, when I look at the clock it's 8 am. I look next to me, and the wife is not there. I yell for her, but there's no answer. She probably made her way to the grocery store. I hurry and get dressed, trying to make it out of the house before she gets home.

As I sit in the car at the parking lot, I'm contemplating on what to say to her. She sells jewelry at Jay's Jewel Shop inside of the mall. Do I go in search of a new watch then ask her out? What if she has a boyfriend? I'll tell her I'm separated from my wife and going through a divorce. Er, maybe this isn't a good idea after all.

Against my better judgement, I walk in. I pass by to Simmon's Suits, and I notice she's at the jewelry counter. It's not busy. I feel my hands shake. I try to calm down. Okay, I'm going to do this. I walk back and enter the shop. I look around until I find the watches. I act interested in them, and that's when she comes over to me. She says, "We have a special, 20% off."

I show her one I like, while we make small talk. I say, "I bet your boyfriend is always buying you nice jewelry. Do you get a work discount?"

She gets all frustrated and shy at the same time. "We broke up last month. I actually broke up with him. He was changing at a rapid pace, but enough about him. Yes, I get a discount."

I lean in with charm on my face and want in my eyes, "How about I take you to Zeniros this Friday?" Then, I point to the most expensive watch, "I'd like to see that one too."

"Oh my gosh, Zeniros?! I heard it takes a month to get in there. I've always wanted to eat there, but it's so pricey." She gets the watch and hands it to me.

I put it on, and with admiration I say, "I'll take it." I hand her my credit card.

After she rings me out, she says, "Yes, I'd love to go with you."

Chapter 10

"Hey, I'm breaking out in a sweat trying to get this meal done before our parents arrive, and you're just sitting there drinking a beer. It's not fair." I'm managing on my own, but I need to blow off some steam. My tension is high, thinking of all four of our parents in the same room. Especially mine, who bluntly say whatever comes to their minds.

"You're doing fine, honey. Is there something you need me to do? I've asked you a dozen times, geez woman, what do you want from me?!" He throws his bottle in the trash and pulls out another beer from the fridge.

"To begin with, a chef would be great. I also need a housekeeper. Not one of those pretty, steal your man away, kind of maids either. I've watched all kinds of movies about that type." I load the breakfast counter with various selections of foods. There's mashed potatoes, gravy, chicken, and carrots to one side. There's cheesecake and banana pudding to the other side.

"Okay, I'll keep my eyes out for an elderly maid that has a wart on her nose. She can do both, cook and clean." He wiggles his eyebrows up and down. "Of course, it could be a problem if I'm looking for a sugar mama."

I put a little bit of mashed potato on the tip of his nose. "I see how you are."

As he twirls me around, there's a knock at the door. We both say in unison, "They're here."

I let go of his hand, "You get the door, and I'll set the table."

I hear him say from the next room, "How did all four of you arrive at the same time? Did you plan it this way?" I can't hear them respond, but I hear, "Mom..." A kiss, "Dad..." I can hear a pat on the back.

I walk into the living room. "What, you can't kiss your father?"

We all exchange hugs and kisses. "I'm so glad you all could make it." I smile at each of them.

"Come into the kitchen. The food is ready!"

Jeremy's dad says, "Great, let's dig in. I'm starving."

His wife, Gwendolyn, says, "Oh Charlie, don't act so hungry. You just had lunch," she looks at her watch, "two hours ago."

My mom, Teresa, laughs and nudges Gwendolyn, "These men eat like horses."

Gwendolyn responds, "Mine shits like one too."

"Mom!" Jeremy shakes his head, as he sets his full plate on the table.

She answers, "Well, he does."

My dad, Henry, changes the topic, "How's work been going for you, Cassie?"

I spoon some mashed potatoes onto my plate, "I couldn't ask for it to be better, Dad. I just closed on three homes."

Mom says, "Three homes? Wow."

Dad grabs a chicken breast, "I'm proud of you, sprout."

Dad and Mom have been calling me sprout for as long as I can remember. When they'd use it in front of my school friends, I'd get embarrassed, but now I find it loving. It's funny how time changes our perspectives.

As we all sit, ready to gobble up our goodies, Jeremy's mom says, "Let's pray."

I close my eyes listening to his mom pray, and I wonder how long it has been since I've prayed. I've been so busy and unthankful to God really. I always want from him, but I never thank him. Every time something bad goes wrong I blame him, but whenever something good happens I go on about life as if he doesn't even exist. Maybe I should develop a closer relationship with God.

Gwendolyn says, "Amen." We all repeat.

She says, "Well, let's all get to eating! It's not going to stay warm forever."

Charlie says, "Jeremy told me you have some good news you wanted to share with us?"

I look over at Jeremy and smile. "Yeah, babe. Tell them!"

Jeremy puts his fork down, holds out a finger to suggest give me a minute, and swallows down his bite of food. He takes a drink of his cola, and then he says, "We decided we're going to buy some property and build a house."

I add in, "Property we already found!!!"

He grins at me, "Yes, property we purchased. It has a river view. It's only 25 miles from here. It's on the other side of town, so we will actually be closer to you all. Not that it matters, any of you are rarely home."

"Now, now son," Gwendolyn says, "When you get older, you'll travel too. You'll see."

Henry says, "Congratulations kids! That's great news! Any idea on the type of house?"

Jeremy answers, "Cassie wants stone and cedar."

My mom says, "That sounds lovely, just lovely!"

I tell her, "You should see the view! It not only has a river, but it has a swimming hole too. It's like a small community in the middle of nowhere."

Jeremy speaks up, "And you don't have to worry about Cassie being there alone when I'm out of town because it's a gated community. Henry raises his glass, "It sounds like a nice dream come true. Don't you think, Teresa?"

My mom looks at my dad with as much love as she did when I was growing up, "It sure does, dear."

I notice how well behaved my parents are today, and it makes me wonder what's up. I ask, "Is there something you want to tell us?" I'm suspicious of them not making any snide or rude comments.

My mom takes a sip of her tea and says, "Now that you mention it, yes. Next week is Henry and my forty-fifth anniversary. We're going on a Caribbean Cruise."

Henry adds in, "Yes, swimming pool, hot tub, dancing, and the finest meals."

I look at my parents and smile. "Sounds like fun Mom and Dad."

Jeremy puts his drink down, "I have never been on a cruise, but I've heard a lot about them. Just be careful."

Charlie looks over at Henry and says, "The only thing you'll have to be careful about is getting fat on their food." We all laugh.

Gwendolyn and my mom help me take the dishes to the sink. "Honey, I don't think your dishwasher will fit all of these. Let us help you clean up."

The men go into the living room and turn the game on. I can hear Jeremy ask them if they want a beer. Both decline, talking about the drive.

My mom says, "Sounds like you have quite a future ahead of you." She gives me a kiss on the back of my head, while I'm soaking some plates.

Gwendolyn says, "If they ever get married, I'd like to have me a grandchild."

My mom's excitement grows, "Oh, a first grandchild! Wouldn't that be great!"

I bite my tongue so hard it hurts. I want to tell them so badly, but it's jumping the gun at this point. I keep the news to myself, as hard as it is.

By the time we're done with the dishes, the men are putting on their coats. Jeremy says, "It was sure good seeing you." He hugs his parents as I hug mine. Then, we exchange and hug each other's parents.

After they leave, I tell Jeremy all about what they said about marriage and a baby and how hard it was to keep my mouth shut about it. He just laughed it off and replied, "Soon enough." I've never kept anything from my parents.

We've always been upfront with each other, but I guess Jeremy is right. What if I can't get pregnant? What if he decides he doesn't want me? What if he gets tired of me?

Jeremy pulls me onto the couch, and we finish the rest of the night with an action movie he said he'd been waiting all week to see.

Chapter 11

The light is creeping in through the curtains, awakening me from a blissful sleep. I turn and look at Jeremy beside me. This feels like such an awesome dream. I lean over and kiss his cheek. Then, I quietly get up and slip into his t-shirt and boxers. I go to the kitchen to wrangle up some breakfast. I notice there is nothing to make. My grocery cart was so full by time I bought last night's dinner. I decide I'll get dressed and go to the store. While I'm out, I'll pick us up some tarts or bagels from the coffee brewery.

I quietly slip into the bedroom. I go to the closet and pick out a long-sleeved spring dress and my boots. Then I tiptoe to the guest bathroom down the hall. I don't need any make-up today. I can just go as I am.

I almost forgot the keys. I slap my forehead and roll my eyes. I grab them and make my way out the door. The drive there was as peaceful as usual. The brewery is pretty quiet, which doesn't surprise me on a Monday morning. Most people are at work by now.

I make my order. As I'm walking away, I remember I forgot the bagels. As I turn, I bump into a man. He looks vaguely familiar. "I'm so sorry!" Luckily, I didn't spill anything on him.

"Well, hello to you too. Er, if you wanted my attention, you could have just said hi." We both laugh.

"Do I know you? You look familiar."

He says, "I get that a lot."

"Ma'am was there something else you needed? You're holding up the line."

I look behind me and realize there's a few people waiting, including the one I bumped in to. I say, "Yes, I need four honey pecan bagels."

As I wait, I turn around, still recognizing the man from somewhere. I can't quite place my finger on it. I know that I know him. I just shake my head, trying to relieve myself of the notion.

I take my seat, waiting for my name to be called. After he orders, he walks over to me, and says, "Has anyone told you that you are a sight for sore eyes? You're absolutely stunning."

I blush, "Awww, thank you. I haven't been complimented since... since... since.... I don't know when."

The guy next to the register calls out, "Cassie. Cassie."

I stand up and retrieve my order. I make my way out the door, and I'm on my way home. I have the music blaring some Wilson Philips. "Yeah, yeah, yeah." Of course, I'm singing right along with them.

When I get out of my car, I wonder if Jeremy is awake yet. I hope not. I really want to surprise him. Shit, I forgot to go to the grocery store. Maybe that's something we can do together.

I walk inside and to my happy elated self, Jeremy is not awake. I pour us some orange juice and coffee. Then, I put the bagels on the breakfast tray alongside of them. I go into the room and put the tray on my side of the bed. I walk over to his side and give him kisses, until his eyes flutter open. "Are you hungry, babe?"

He stretches, "What time is it?"

"It's 11 am. Did I wake you too soon?"

"No, no." He sits up and sees the tray. "Ah, breakfast in bed."

"I was going to the store, but by the time I finished at the coffee brewery I forgot. Do you want to go with me later? If not, I thought I could go tomorrow, while you're at work."

"No need for the grocery store today. I want to take you out! I want to celebrate the property we now own."

I bend over and give him a kiss. Then, I walk back over and sit on my side of the bed. I pull the tray toward us, and we enjoy our breakfast together.

He says, "I want all wooden floors. I hate carpet. I think it holds so many allergens."

"Only if you promise to buy me a lifetime of furry socks or house shoes."

He laughs and agrees, "Anything you want beautiful."

I ask him, "Are you full?" I look forward to spending the day with him. For a while, we were both so busy we barely had time for a quick kiss on the way out the door!

He nods, and I carry the tray back to the kitchen. I start the dishes, while he showers. I play with my name change when I get married, then I just laugh at myself for feeling like a teenager. I can't believe I'm having a dream house built, going to get married, and have Jeremy's baby! I hope she has his big eyes. Wow, did I say she?! If I had a little girl I could play with her hair and dress her up so cute. On the other hand, if I had a little boy he could carry on our family's name. Jeremy could play sports with him. Either way, I'm happy.

"Hon?" Jeremy pinches my waist. "You were in lala land."

"I was just thinking about having a baby with you. I'd be happy with either gender. Is there one you're particularly hoping for?"

He smiles at me, "I want either, as long as it looks like you."

"Actually, I was just hoping it'll have your big, round, brown eyes."

"Hey, do you want to go to my office with me and look over some plans of houses? We can even check out a few display models and get some ideas."

I cover my mouth with my hand, all giddy, "Really?! I'd love to."

An hour later and we're driving to his office. It's not a huge building. Nothing in this town is. We have a mall, but it's all one floor. Our hospital is the biggest building around. We go up to the third floor, and sure enough all along his wall are different designs of buildings.

He says, "Take a seat." He pulls out a portfolio of different designs. "I know it's not easy getting an idea of what it will look like, so I thought you could search through some floor plans. If you see any you like I can get the keys from downstairs, and we can look at the display models at different subdivisions."

"Sure, but you know me... if I see one I like, I get my heart set on it."

"And that's one of your best qualities, babe."

We go through the plans for about an hour, when I see one that has a fireplace that sticks out on its own from the side. It has a sitting room, a dining room, a wraparound bar in a huge kitchen. It has four bedrooms, a finished walk out basement, and an extra two bedrooms downstairs. "I like this, and we can make the two bedrooms downstairs into our offices."

He comes around the desk and looks over my shoulder, "You sure you don't want a two-story?"

"I don't think it's wise with having children. Do you?"

He answers, "They do it all the time." He takes the design. "Okay, and I like this one. It's a two-story with a finished basement. Why don't we look at both today?" He puts them both in a folder. "Oh, and honey, don't be disappointed if the outsides aren't stone and cedar. We will have that done ourselves. I'm not sure what kind of siding they have." He makes his way downstairs to retrieve the keys while I wait for him. I put my jacket back on.

I hear, "Come on, honey. I got them. Let's go."

We decide to go to mine first, and to my surprise it has

stone and cedar siding!!! The outside is huge for being one-story. We go inside and it has high ceilings, which kind of worries me. It's hard to change light bulbs without hiring someone. On the other hand, it gives it a more spacious environment. We walk into a small foyer with a coat closet. "Nice," I say. It has tiles on the floor. Then, we walk through to a huge living room that opens into a dining room. "Oh my gosh! Look at the fireplace, honey." It's a three-way view. It shows the living room, the dining room, and then out toward the kitchen.

We walk past the kitchen, into a hall that leads us past a small den. This worried me because I thought it would mean the bedrooms were small. I was wrong. All four bedrooms are huge. There are two suites with bathrooms in them. The other two bedrooms are adjoined by a Jack and Jill bathroom. "This is so beautiful. I'm not sure I want to leave."

He takes my hand, "Come on, babe. We still have to see the basement." I follow his lead.

We go back through the wood floor living room to a carpeted staircase. "Uh-oh, I say."

"Actually, I don't mind the stairs having carpet. This way we don't slip." We get downstairs, and it's one huge family room. They have like an 85-inch television screen and a sectional couch that wraps around the TV. "In here," he yells.

I walk down a hall, and into one of the bedrooms. "Wow, this will be plenty of room for you to have your sofa and desk. If we work, the kids can play in the family room. We can make it a toy room." I go into the second office, and there's a huge picture window. "This one is mine," I call out.

We meet back in the family room. "It has a sliding door, babe." He unlocks it, and we walk out to the backyard. "Even better yet, we can also watch the dogs from our office windows." From the back it looks like a two-story house.

"I'm so excited. I really like this one, Jeremy. Don't worry, I'm still willing to give yours a chance."

"Nope, if you like this one, then this one it will be! I want to get moving on these plans, so we can get married and start our family."

"Can't you just see it, honey? I sure can."

He leans down and gives me a kiss and says, "Yes, yes I do."

"Come on now, let's get us something to eat."

Chapter 12

I can't believe I saw my dream gal today and didn't say more. What was I thinking?! I finish trimming the bushes, while still feeling mad at myself. I think I'll ask the wife for a divorce. The kids are almost finished with school. Divorces happen all the time. Their kids seem fine. Mine will too. I know my gal will want to get married. I'll be able to give her so much more than I was able to give the old nag that's never satisfied. I bet she'll be appreciative.

Tonight, I have a date with Alicia. I'll find out all kinds of information about my dream gal. I need a plan without looking conspicuous. Too many questions might get Alicia jealous, and I don't want that. It's a fine dining restaurant, so I'll need to wear a suit. I bet she'll look amazing, but she's not the one I want.

I finish up with the trimming and start mowing the lawn. By the time I'm done, it's dusk. I better get in and tidy up. It's almost time for my date. I'll just tell the wife I have a late appointment. That's the good thing about working with annuities in insurance, there's no set schedule!

After I'm done showering and changing, I put on some cologne the wife bought me last Christmas. At least, she has good taste in that. I take a glance in the mirror. I'm satisfied with who I see. I look for my keys and can't find them anywhere. "Damn it, where are my keys?" I walk into the kitchen to ask the wife.

She says, "How would I know!"

I roll my eyes, "Because you clean. Maybe you picked

them up and put them somewhere."

She puts her hand on her hip, "If I did, I'd tell you where they are!"

"Whatever," I look around some more until I find them in the bedroom on the nightstand. "I'll be out late tonight. I have a few appointments. Don't wait up."

It's raining out, so when I get to my car, I'm splattered on. I should have brought an umbrella to hold over Alicia. I wasn't thinking, and I'm not going to backtrack now. I'll be even wetter than I already am. The drive to her apartment was fairly simple. It was probably thirty minutes away from my house.

I look at the intercom and ring number three. "Hello," a voice answers back.

"It's me. I'm here to pick you up for our date," I shift weight from one leg to another. I think to myself, come on already, it's raining.

She says, "I'll be down in a minute."

I respond, "Okay."

Her minute felt more like five. As I was getting ready to walk back to the car, where I could stay dry, she comes outside. She's wearing heels, which makes it pretty slippery for her. "Hi," I say. "You look stunning." I take her arm to help her down the stairs.

She looks down to her high heels and back up to me, "Oh, thanks so much. You look quite handsome yourself."

I open the door for her to get in. "I'm starving."

"Now you're reading my mind," she answers, as she puts on her seat belt.

She's a pretty woman. She has long, red hair. I can tell it's natural. She has the freckles to match. Her eyes are both big and blue. She appears to be all legs. I like that in a woman. If it weren't for my dream gal, I'd snatch this one up and make her mine instead! Too bad for her I'm already taken. Of course, she doesn't know that, and she doesn't need to know it.

"Well, that was a fast drive." She starts to open her door.

"Hold on, I'll get that for you, madam." I make my way to her side of my car. I open her door and take her hand. She tells me, "I heard Zeniros has the best food around."

We get inside and make small talk. I decide to bring up my best friend, Calvin. Even though there is no Calvin, maybe that will make her think of her best friend. Unfortunately, it did nothing for me. She's still going on and on about her sick mother. How she takes care of her, and the rest is kind of blank. I tuned her out. She says, "Enough about me, how about you?"

I'm not getting what I need from this bitch, which makes this all a waste of time. I'm getting to the end of my nerves, when I say, "I don't think this is working out, Alicia." I really don't want to talk about myself. I want to hear everything there is to know about her best friend. It doesn't seem to sink into her thick skull! I wouldn't mind crushing it right about now.

She quietly remarks, "Okay." She doesn't finish her dinner. She just looks down at her plate.

I continue to look over at her, "Shall we call it a night?"

We get to my car, and I start driving her home. She says, "This isn't the way to my place."

I explain, "I want to show you somewhere before I take you home. I think you'll find it beautiful."

She says, "If it's not working out, what's the point? Please, just take me home."

I pull over to the side of the road. I lean over and wrap my hands tightly around her neck. She never shuts up. I choke her into silence. Finally she's quiet. I strangle her until I see her try to take her very last breath. Then I drive to the conservation park. I don't like the spot very much because it probably has a lot of park rangers. I'll have to be selective. I wear driving gloves during the spring, especially in the rain, so at least I don't have to worry about my fingerprints being on her.

Chapter 13

"The dinner went well with our parents, don't you think?" Jeremy inquires, as I put the dishes up the next morning.

"Yes, I was surprised mine were on such good behavior." I close the cabinet door.

Jeremy laughs, "Because your mom doesn't admit your dad shits like a horse?" I add in my laugh too. "They seem really excited about our house being closer to theirs."

"Oh my God, it was so hard not to tell them we plan on getting married there and starting a family. Our moms were really on me about it. It was almost to the point where I told."

"But you didn't, and that's what matters." Jeremy starts helping me. He puts the pot and pan away. "It's all going to come along for the greater good."

I wipe down the counter, "You sound like a sales representative now."

"The house is going to be built faster than you think. We should start packing little by little. Do you think we should throw a going away party or a housewarming party?"

I answer, "Well, since we're going to be having our wedding there, I think it would be a good idea to throw a going away party. Otherwise, the housewarming party and the wedding will be too much." I rinse the rag and put it in the sink. "By the way, what are you going to do with the dogs during the wedding?"

He says, "I've thought a lot about that. I plan on putting them in a boarding school. Before you have a fit, they'll have lots of fun. I'll show you the brochure. It even has cameras in their pens. After, we'll have the yard cleaned up. That way if people want to step outside, we don't have to worry about them stepping in dog shit."

I let out a nervous giggle, "Sounds good to me. I'd like to see the brochure ASAP, though."

He goes into his office to retrieve it, while I wipe down the kitchen table. It felt kind of crowded at our circular table, but soon we'll have a big dining room. No more crowded space!!! I start to get excited all over again.

"I can't wait to see my friends. It feels like forever. I've been so busy selling houses I haven't had the time."

He walks back into the kitchen, "Here it is." He holds out the brochure.

I look hesitant, "It could be false advertisement."

"Except the fact they told me to stop in anytime and get a tour. They said their work gang is there every day."

I take the pamphlet from him and browse through it. "I'll miss them so much."

"Honey," he says, "it's not going to be for that long. One day. It's not like we're jumping straight to a honeymoon, although it would be a perfect time to."

He looks at me as if it just entered his mind. I pinch his side, "We better get the house and the wedding paid for first. Besides, being in a new house will be like a honeymoon. Then we need to save up for who?????"

He grabs me in his arms and lifts me off the floor, "A baby!" I look down and kiss him before he puts me back down.

I agree, "That's right, a baby." I take in a deep breath and slowly exhale. Then I ask, "How long do you think before the house is done?"

He says, "They've already started working on it. I have a whole team. I'd say about two months."

"Two months is plenty of time to start packing. It's not like we have to start right away." I feel a load of stress come off my shoulders. "The way you were talking, I thought it was just weeks away."

"Most homes take much longer, but since ours is a one-story, and you happen to know the designer." He smiles. "It'll be a lot less time."

"It has its perks." I sit on the couch and rest, as I browse some more through the pamphlet. "It says they have an obstacle course that they have the dogs run each day. Ours would love that."

He adds in, "Did you see where it says they go for a nature hike each day? They also go to a dog park where they all get to play with each other."

I feel skeptical, "What if there are unruly, mean dogs there?"

He smiles at me then says, "Leave our dogs out of this."

I throw a small couch pillow at him. "I'm serious, Jeremy."

"If you read the back, it says they've been a family operated business for twenty-five years. They know how to handle things. Stop worrying so much, babe."

I chew on my nail, "Wow, they even have a dog pool. There's always a chance they may not want to return home."

"Well, that's too bad. They're stuck with us!" We both look over at the three dogs. Two are sleeping, and the other is playing with his unstuffed monkey toy.

I get up and go into the kitchen for a drink of water. I yell out, "Alicia may have disowned me. It's been forever since we've talked."

Jeremy says, "That works both ways. When's the last time she's called?"

"Well, let's see. I believe when she was hired at the jewelry shop."

He looks puzzled, "That was over a year ago?"

"I told you, it's been a while." I kick my feet up on the coffee table.

"A while and a year... okay." He lies his head on my lap,

and I play with his hair. "You two used to be so close."

"Best friendships never die out. I'll call her. Maybe we can have lunch next week. Now that I've closed on the three houses, I have some time." I pull a loch of hair.

"Ow, meanie."

I ask, "What about you? When's the last time you've been out with friends?"

He answers, "Actually, about a month ago. I met up with Mike and Tony." He sits back up. "We had lunch, caught up to where we are in life, and talked sports."

I grab onto a pillow, "How come I didn't know about this?"

"I mentioned it, but you were pretty busy. Maybe you let it go in one ear and out the other."

I say, "Hey now." I start to feel really guilty for not calling Alicia. I'd also like to talk to Rose. Maybe the three of us can meet up for lunch. "I'm going to call Rose tomorrow too. I bet she'd like to have lunch with us."

"Us?" He reaches for the remote. "Does that mean I'm invited?"

"No way, it's chick's day! No good-looking men invited."

He flips through the channels, "Are you saying if I was ugly, I could go?"

I just shake my head. "Stop being so silly."

He says, "Remember when we tried setting Alicia up with Mike? That was a complete disaster."

"Yeah, but we would have never known had we not tried," I think back, "We should get brownie points for that."

He stops at Dukes of Hazard, "Two people couldn't have been more different."

"Hey, it was your idea!"

He mutes the TV, "I never denied it." Then he turns the volume back up. "Do you want to watch this with me?"

"Sure," I take the couch cover and pull it over us and lean back on the couch.

Chapter 14

"You weren't lying when you said you were going to wear jeans to work. Your ass looks too good in those. Maybe you should start wearing baggies." I wink at Jeremy.

"I can't believe I'm running this late. I was supposed to meet with the contractor an hour ago."

"Honey, can't you just call them?" I try to make light of the situation to calm his nerves. I can tell how stressed he is. "And is this concerning our house or the creek place?"

He runs his fingers through his hair, "Our place, which is why it's even more important for me to be there." He picks up his cell phone. "Yeah, don't leave. I'm on my way."

I give Jeremy a kiss as he's leaving, then I take the three dogs to the backyard. "Fetch boys, fetch!"

Colombo Columbus takes off first. This is unusual for him, but he's getting better by the day. He was shy and aloof when I brought him home from the rescue center. He had been treated poorly in his previous home. He was always on a chain through snow, rain and sleet. Poor baby! Now he's spoiled rotten, and he's loving living with us.

I grab the rope and run. "Can't get me boys, can't get me." All three chase me around the yard. I play with them, until my body won't let me. I've worn myself out. "Let's go in and get a drink." They follow me in. I fill the boys water bowl, then I go into the kitchen to find something for myself. I pull out a Powerade. "You guys stay inside, while I go to the grocery store." I have time to go before feeding them their dinner. I need to pick up a bag of dog food as well.

After I shower, I just throw on my comfortable grey sweats and a sweater. No need to dress up for the grocery store. I throw my hair up in a ponytail, put on some lip gloss, and I'm out the door. The three dogs were napping because they can't keep up with me. I smile to myself.

The drive there was relaxing as usual. The parking lot is packed. Everybody in town must be here today. I drive around, until I see a Camry pulling out. Great, right up front too! My phone rings, "Hello?"

"Yes, my name is Molly Anderson. You were referred to me by my friend Sarah. I'm hoping to trouble you into finding a condo for me. I'm single, so I think a condo will do just fine for now."

I always love the words, for now. That means if I do a good job now, later my clients will come back to me when they're ready for a step bigger. "Oh, Sarah! She's a sweetheart. We go way back. As for a condo, there are only a handful on the market right now. There aren't a lot of condos in town. However, we can take a look at a couple I know off-hand."

She shrills with delight, "Can we look at them tomorrow?"

I pull in the spot, "We sure can. I'll see you tomorrow, Miss Anderson." I can tell she sounds like she's in her twenties, if that."

"Please, just call me Molly."

Already the day is going well. I had a few extra hours with Jeremy, played with the dogs, and now I have a prospective buyer. I walk into the store with a skip in my walk. That's when I see Sarah. Talk about coincidence. "Sarah?!"

"Oh, hi Cassie! We were just talking about you last night."

"This is such a coincidence. I just got off the phone with Molly Anderson. We were just talking about you!" I grab a grocery cart. I look inside hers and see she's already pulled a case of water from the stack. I say, "It's a good thing I saw your water, or I may have forgotten mine."

She looks down at her water and then back up at me, "Don't you hate that! I especially hate when I come into the store for something specific and walk out with everything but that!"

I nod, "I've done that one too many times."

"Well, I better get what I need and get back home to Wayne, before he starts wondering where I am."

I touch her shoulder, "Wait. Before you leave, I was going to let you know next month Jeremy and I are throwing a moving out party. Do you want to come?"

"Moving out?! Where are you moving to?"

I tell her about the place we found at River's Hill. I go on about how we're going to build a home there. I almost said and plan a family, but I quickly stopped myself.

"Sure, Wayne and I will be there. It sounds like fun! Do you need me to bring anything?"

"We'll have plenty to drink, and we're ordering a ton of pizza. So, the only thing we ask, is if you want dessert, bring it. If not, don't worry about it."

We smile, and she journey's ahead of me, stopping at the tomatoes. I am reminded that when I get home, I need to call Alicia and Rose. Let's see... Alicia is, or was, single. Rose is married. That will make 2, 4, 5 people I've invited. I better let Jeremy pick out the rest before I over crowd us.

By the time I'm done grocery shopping, once again my cart is packed. I go to the checkout, which I dread, and pull everything out of the cart. As an elderly lady is paying ahead of me, she is five dollars short. She's trying to find some money in her wallet. I offer to pay for it instead. "Here you go." I hand it to the clerk.

The elderly lady says, "That's mighty nice of you."

I smile at her, and explain, "I've had it happen to me quite a few times." I put the orange juice on the counter. I think I have everything when I notice a gravy pouch stuck against the cart. I grab it and put it on the counter too. I go to the end and start putting bags in the cart, as she rings up the rest of the items.

She says, "That's $67.86."

I charge it to my MasterCard. Now, as I walk to the car, I dread it. Putting everything in the trunk, just to get home and take it all out, carry it in, then put it all away. It's crazy. I guess I shouldn't complain, though. At least we're doing well enough to be able to do this.

After I get home and unload the groceries, I pick up my phone and dial Alicia. It rings, but then goes straight to voicemail like it either ran out of charge, or she's on the other line. I leave a message, telling her how sorry I am I haven't called and about the party.

Then, I call Rose. It rings a few times before she picks up, "Hello?"

"Rose! It's so good to hear your voice. I know it's been a while, but it's me Cassie!"

Her voice raises an octave, "Cassie?! Oh my God, it's good to hear you too!"

"Sorry it's been a while, but I've been so busy in real estate. I just closed three houses, and now I'm looking into a condominium for another client. Do you want to have lunch tomorrow and catch up? I thought I'd invite Alicia too. I tried calling her earlier, but I got her voicemail."

"That's weird. I tried calling her a few times yesterday, and I got the same thing. Sure, I'd love to have lunch with you. When and where?"

"Let's do the coffee brewery." I catch my breath, "Best coffee in town."

"Okay, great. See you tomorrow, Cassie."

I hang up and try dialing Alicia. Same thing again. Almost directly to voicemail.

Maybe I should stop by her condo on the way home. I need to check on one near her anyway, for Molly. I pay the bill, walk to my car, and I get an eerie feeling. It's almost as if I'm being watched. I look around and see nobody paying any attention to me. "Weird."

I pull up to her place, and I don't see her car. Maybe she's still at work. I don't even bother knocking because if she were home her car would be here. I make my way home. On the way, I call Jeremy, "Hey, babe. I made lunch plans with Rose and tried calling Alicia again, but it went straight to voicemail. Sooo, I stopped by her condo, and her car isn't there. Anyway, I'm making my way home, just in case you get there before I do. Love you."

As I pull in our drive, I see the three dogs outside. Aha, he did make it home before I did. I walk inside and throw my purse on the couch, "I'm wore out. I didn't even really do anything, and I feel exhausted."

He stirs the pot, "Thought we'd have some beef stew." He opens the lid, and the aroma coming from the pot smells delicious. He says, "Do you think you're coming down with something?"

"I don't think I'm sick. I haven't been around anyone that showed any kind of symptoms. I just feel tired." I go into the bedroom and change out of my skirt and into a t-shirt and some loose, sweat material shorts.

I sit on the couch and cuddle with my pillow and cover. I grab the remote, flipping through the channels, when Jeremy walks in. "What's the matter? You look sad."

"I'm worried about Alicia." I take the bowl of soup he's holding out for me. "It's not like her not to call me back."

"Leave early and swing by her work tomorrow morning. I'm sure she's fine. Maybe take a peek at rings." He winks at me.

"Oh right!!! Perfect opportunity to see Alicia. She'll be excited when I tell her what for." I smile, feeling better now than I did before. "I love you," I give Jeremy a kiss. "You're always here to brighten my day."

He takes a spoonful of stew, "I love you too, and that's what I'm here for, to make you feel better than you would without me."

Chapter 15

I followed her to the coffee brewery. She met up with another woman. I'm not sure who she is, but you're damned right I'm going to find out. Maybe it's her that I can get some information from. So, I went slowly behind her as she drove home. She lives in an apartment building, which makes it even more complex. I stayed put until nightfall, when I saw her leave with whom I assumed is her husband. The reason I say husband is, I did notice at the brewery she was wearing a ring. I need to find out where she works. How am I going to get her to give me information? Er, what if she doesn't work?! Since she's married, I can't sweet talk using my charm. These are dynamics I'm going to have to work out.

By the time I get home it's late, but I can't sleep. I toss and turn, before realizing it's not working. I get in the closet and pull out a blanket and take it to the couch. I haven't watched television in quite a while. Usually, I'm too busy.

I find a black and white comedy that already has me laughing. Before I know it, I'm out like a light. By the time I open my eyes, the wife is in the kitchen frying what smells like eggs and bacon. I quickly grab my watch off the coffee table. "Nine o'clock," I have to go! "I don't have time for breakfast."

"I'm still making it for the kids." She says sarcastically, "You're not the only one who eats around here."

I go to the bedroom and change my clothes. Once I look all snazzy, I do my favorite thing, leave. "I'll be back later to work more in the backyard." Slowly but surely, I'm getting it all done. Next, is the BBQ area, and I still need to weed eat.

I pop in the office briefly. "Hi, Sue."

She looks up from a heavy stack of papers, "Oh, hi. I didn't see you over this Mount Everest I have compiling." She smiles and nods her head towards the paper stack.

I go to the back and look through my client's list on the computer. A few bills are due, so I take a couple pictures of their addresses with my phone's camera. I'll stop by and see if they want to make a payment to me, to save them the hassle of trying to mail it in on time. If they're not home, then it's not because I didn't try.

The first address I go to, I stand in front of the door and knock. The house is battered and old. You can tell it has been through quite a few families. "Hello?" I call in through the screen door.

A short elderly lady with thick glasses says, "Hello! Can I help you?" She's walking hunched over with a cane in her hand, helping to steady her.

I explain to her that I'm from the insurance company and that her annuity is due. I ask if she'd prefer to pay me instead of trying to mail it in on time, since I'm already here. I tell her if she prefers to mail it, that's fine too.

She invites me in. "Would you like something to drink? Perhaps some tea?" She goes into her dimly lit kitchen that has more outside light coming in than what's showing through her light bulbs.

"No thank you, ma'am." I get my card out and proof of reputability. Though, she didn't ask for it, later she can rest assured when she thinks about it.

"I'm not getting any younger," she says, as she makes some noises as she sits down. "I come with sound effects and all. You're still too young to know all about that." She takes a drink of her tea, then sits it down on the coffee table. She gets her purse next to the couch and takes out her wallet. "And how much is it again?"

As I give her a quote, she says, "Oh yes. Here it is on last month's check. Silly me. I went right past it." She writes me out a check, then I say my goodbye.

At the second address, a bald man comes to the door. "What do you want?"

Again, I explain why I'm there and tell him he can pay if he'd like or mail it in. It's his choice. He also invites me in. "Have a seat," he says, all too grizzly. He doesn't offer me anything to drink, which is sad. My throat is getting dry, and I think this time I would have accepted it.

He passes me cash and says, "I didn't know you did house calls."

"Well, typically I'm in the office to call out reminders, but I've been otherwise preoccupied. So, I decided to make house calls." I put the cash in an envelope and stick it in my briefcase. I write out a receipt, hand it to him, then say, "Have a good day." I show myself out the door.

Before I know it, I'm at the apartment I followed my dream gal's friend from yesterday. I check my watch, and it's almost lunch time. I never see her come out, but soon I see her husband. I follow with a distance behind him. He goes up to the second-floor apartment 201. "201," I say to myself. Then I leave.

I stop off at the lumber company again to get more concrete blocks, so that we can add a small patio underneath the BBQ area. Next, we'll add some tables. First things first! I'm in a good mood. I whistle, as I go through the store toward the back, where the garden area is. The young guy there helps me put the concrete blocks into the cart. I ask, "Do you think you could help me unload these in my car?"

"Sure, I can also check you out over here."

I pull out my billfold and pay. Before I know it, I'm on my way home. I drive to the back where the garage is, and I park lopsided. I debate doing this today. I already feel tired. Then, the thought of going inside makes me feel sick. So, I unload the car. I stack the cement blocks by the BBQ area. Next, I go to the garage and pull out the weed eater.

An hour later and the weed eating is finished. I look over at the blocks, still contemplating. I hear the wife call out, "Dinner is ready." I'm starving.

I go inside and see she's made a roast. "Smells good," I tell her, as I pull a plate from the stack on the counter. "I got the weed eating done. I think I'll try to get some blocks down tonight."

She says, "It really looks good out there." She pats my back.

Her fingers feel like ice. It's like a creepy witch running her fingers down your back. I get the chills.

The kids come in, after making their plates, they sit with us at the table. The wife says, "This is the first time we've had a family dinner in quite some time. Usually, we're missing a few of you." She smiles with a pleased look on her face.

Later, I'm getting on the computer and doing a cross reference on her apartment and phone number. Maybe I can talk to her about insurance. She might be interested in an annuity. We could talk business. She might bring up her friend casually. I'll ask for references. That might open her up.

"Dinner was good," I say, as I make my way to the office. I look up the address and see a name. Rose Welch. I then go to the site that has the white pages. I look up Rose Welch, and sure enough, a phone number comes up. I dial it, and she answers.

"Rose here."

"Hi, Rose! I'm from," I think of a name really quick in case she has time to talk to her husband before I have a chance to get there, "Pearson's Annuity."

She says, "Pearson's Annuity, I've never heard of it."

"I was wondering if I could set up a meeting with you to go over some paperwork to see if you'd want to learn about us. We've been in business for over thirty years. We also offer retirement plans."

"Wow, I was just talking about retiring and how we

haven't figured anything out. Sure, I'd like to see you. How about this evening at 7 pm?"

I get her address and feel satisfied. I wonder if her husband will be there.

I take a shower and quickly change. I go through the papers in my briefcase, prepping it for tonight's meeting. Out with the old and in with the new. I crush some old papers in my hand and throw it in the trash bin. No need for those anymore.

When I get to her apartment, I stand there for a few minutes. I can hear voices coming through her door. Her husband must be home. I run my fingers through my hair and knock.

"Hi! I'm the insurance agent that called earlier." I move my briefcase forward, she moves to the side, letting me in.

"This is my husband, Christopher. You can call him Chris." Chris holds his hand out, and I shake it. He points to the couches and says, "Please, have a seat."

I put my briefcase on the coffee table and open it. "So, your wife tells me you have no idea for a retirement plan?"

Chris says, "Not really."

We go over all the details, and I explain to him about the trust too. He seems rather taken by it. He says, "Let me look this over, and I'll get back to you as soon as possible."

"Do you have any friends that might be interested as well?" I ask, when Rose walks back in from the kitchen and passes me a glass of water.

Rose looks over at Chris. "Do you think Cassie and Jeremy might be interested?"

"If you have a phone number, I can contact them and ask. I never harass or call continuously. Just once, to see if there's interest or not."

Rose gives me their home phone number, and I leave feeling satisfied.

Chapter 16

"I can't believe I still haven't heard from Alicia. I'm going to call her work." I slide the cell phone out of my blazer's pocket.

It rings a few times, "Jay's Jewelers. Kaden speaking."

"Hi, my name is Cassie Jennings. I'm looking for Alicia. I'm a close friend of hers."

Kaden gets quiet and then says, "We haven't heard from Alicia in quite a few days now. She's pretty close to losing her job."

I ask, "Do you know when the last time she was in?"

She says, "I'm not supposed to tell you this," her voice gets quieter, "A little under a week ago."

I let out a sigh, "And she hasn't called in?"

"No word from her at all."

I respond, "Okay, thanks."

Jeremy sees the worry in my eyes and asks, "What's the matters, hon?"

"It's been a week since they've seen or heard from Alicia." I open a jar of pickles. "That's not like her. I know it's been a while since we've talked, but she's always been the responsible one." I take a bite, and as I chew, I say, "I'm going by her condo today while I'm close by. Maybe this time her car will be there. If not, I'm calling her mom after my scheduled appointment with Molly Anderson." I take a final crunch of the pickle.

Jeremy responds, "Okay, chewy." He gives me a kiss on the forehead. "We will see each other later then."

I let the three dogs back in. "I'll be home soon. You be good."

On my way to Alicia's, I wonder if I should go ahead and call her mom, but the traffic is pretty heavy today. Which is unusual on this county road! I get to Alicia's, and her car still isn't there. What the hell is going on!

I go to the condo in the subdivision to the left of Alicia's. I get out of my car and notice Molly looking through a window. She meets me on the sidewalk between the lawn. She holds out her hand, "I'm Molly. You must be Cassie."

"You're right! Nice to meet you."

After giving Molly a tour of a few condos, she finds one she really likes. She says, "I love living in the city. There's so much more to do and see than when I lived in the country with my parents."

"Well, I'll call them as soon as I get to my office." I wanted to say home, but that sounds less professional. "I'm glad you found a place you are happy with."

On my way back to the car, I call Alicia's mom, Sandy. It rings a few times, then I hear, "Hello?"

"Sandy, this is Callie. I've been trying to reach Alicia, and she hasn't responded. That's not like her. Have you heard from her?"

Sandy clears her throat and says, "No, and when I found out her car has been at the mall this whole time, I filed a missing person's report. I tried finding your number, so I could call you. I didn't have any luck. So, I called the few friends I did find."

"Yeah, it seems strange. If she were with her friends, it wouldn't be for this long. She's close to losing her job. Her car's parked at the mall? None of it makes any sense. I feel really bad because I haven't talked with her in a long time." I put the phone to my other ear. "Has she been dating anyone new?"

She answers, "Not that she's told me, but it had been a few days since we last spoke. I miss her so much. I just hope they find her soon."

I get off the phone with her mother, and I drive to the mall. I try to open the door, but it's locked. I peer through the windows and look for anything suspicious, but I don't see anything out of place. Alicia always kept her car immaculate. Maybe if I go inside the jeweler shop, I can get more information from the workers. Maybe if I go to the police station, I can get some posters of Alicia and put them up around town. Or if they don't have them, I can offer to make some. I feel so helpless.

I pick the phone back up and dial Rose. "Did you hear Sandy, Alicia's mom, filed a missing person's report?"

She says, "I just found out today when I called her. I can't think of anywhere else she would be. She's not the type to up and leave."

I respond, "No, she's definitely not. Okay, I better start driving home because I have a contract to call in. Rose, if you hear anything more about Alicia, please call me."

"Will do! You do the same. Talk to you later, Cassie."

I want to cry. My best friend is missing, and none of us have any idea what happened. I feel a hallow spot deep down in my chest. The drive home was rather quick. I go inside and check on the three dogs. Then, I go to my bedroom and open my laptop. As I'm filling out the paperwork for the condominium, I can't get Alicia off my mind.

I call Alicia's mom back. "Sandy, did they search her car?"

Sandy says, "They did. They didn't find anything. No fingerprints, no sign of where she might have gone."

"Okay, sorry for bothering you. If you hear anything, can you take down my number and call me?"

I give her my phone number and click end. I hear the front door open. "Jeremy, is that you?"

"Of course, it's me. Who else would be brave enough to enter with your three gallant dogs?"

I run in and give him a hug. "Just hold me."

He fingers some hair out of my face, "What's the matter, babe?"

"Alicia's car is still at the mall. It's been there for a little under a week. Her mom filled out a missing person's report with the police. Nobody has heard from her. It's scary." I take in a quick breath and wipe away a tear that escaped. "I can't imagine where she'd be, and agree with Rose, she's not the type to just leave."

"Oh honey, I'm so sorry. You must be scared out of your mind for her. Have they checked the jewelry store to see if Alicia could have possibly mentioned going somewhere or seeing someone?" He releases me and takes his sweater off, then wraps his arms around me again.

I wrap my arms around him too, "Well, I thought about stopping by there, but I had a contract to write. So, I came straight home instead. After talking to Alicia's mom, it was so much to take in that I just needed to get home and cry."

"Does Alicia have a cabin or some other place else she might have gone?"

"No, and her car is at the mall. It's just all so weird."

We let go of each other, and Jeremy walks into the kitchen. He pours us both a glass of water. "Here." He hands it to me.

"Do you think I should call the police and find out if they have any information yet?" I take a gulp of water and almost choke on it. "Maybe ask them some questions?"

"I doubt they'd give you any information because you're not immediate family. Also, if they had any new information, they would have told Alicia's mom... who would have told you." He takes in a deep breath, "You should go sit on the couch and relax."

I tell him, "I can't. I still have to finish writing the contract for the condominium. Molly found one she likes. Remind me later to invite Sarah and Wayne over for dinner. She recommended me to Molly."

He joins me on the couch and says, "Sure thing."

Chapter 17

"I don't have to go to the job site today. Do you want to go look at rings?" Jeremy is standing in the kitchen and rinses the last dish.

"Why don't you just put it in the dishwasher?" I open it, showing him it's empty.

He dries his hands and puts the towel on his shoulder, as he starts making his way to the bedroom. "It's faster this way, and are you purposely avoiding the question about the ring?"

I yell in, "Hey, bring the hand towel back."

"I'm going to throw it in the wash with the rest of the towels."

I smile, thinking of him doing the laundry for once. "About the ring. Don't you think we should wait for Alicia?"

He yells back, "Not to sound harsh, but baby, this is about us."

"Okay," I bite my lip fully aware I'm going to ask them more questions about Alicia.

I go into the bedroom and see him changing his clothes. He puts on jeans with a dress shirt. I ask, "What do you wear when ring shopping?"

He says, "Something casual and comfortable."

I look around my closet. "I have nothing to wear these days." I browse through the shelf items. "Nothing but shorts, and it's still too cold outside for them."

"What about that blue, spring dress I like so much?"

"Right, that's perfect." I walk over to him and give him a

kiss. "What would I do without you?"

"Well, you wouldn't need a blue, spring dress to go ring shopping in." He laughs.

Then I'm reminded about the shoes and purse. I'll have to go the garage later and see if I can locate the purse. Unless... "Honey, could you help me with the boxes in the garage, so I can see if my handbag is in one of them?"

He puts his vest on, "Babe, I'm dressed and it's dusty in there. Wouldn't you rather do that when we get home and we're dressed more suited for the occasion?"

"Listen to you, making it all sound so fancy." I look over at my flats and slip them on. "Sure, we can do it then."

The whole drive there we talk about the house we'll be in before we know it. How well it's going! We go over what type of countertops I want. He says, "On the way home, we can stop by the tile store and look through some samples."

We get to the mall, and I show him where Alicia's car is parked. We find a parking spot close to it. This time it's Jeremy peeking into the windows. "Looks untouched."

We go inside the mall, passing a few stores, until we get to Jay's Jewelry. I see a young girl helping a customer. She appears to be the only one here. While she's busy, Jeremy and I go to the wedding ring section. I hear her voice and recognize it from our phone conversation. It's Kaden, the girl I talked to over the phone.

Jeremy points out a few sets of rings he likes. I tell him one is too gaudy for my taste, but I really like the other one he picked.

"Hi, I'm Kaden. Is there something I can help you with?"

Jeremy explains, "Actually, my fiancé and I want to look at rings."

Fiancé, I'm still not used to that, but I love the way he says it. "Hi Kaden. I'm Cassie, Alicia's friend, we talked on the phone. Remember me?"

She says, "I do. Congratulations on getting married! With all that's going on, it's uplifting news."

I ask, "All that's going on?"

She leans in closer to us, "The police were just here getting store receipts from us last week when Alicia was working." Then she lowers her voice even more, "They said if someone suspicious bought something maybe they'll have a lead."

Jeremy speaks up, "I'd like to see this set of wedding rings, please." He gives a serious look to us both. He's letting me know I'm supposed to be looking at wedding rings.

I slip the engagement and wedding ring on. "I really love this, Jeremy."

He holds out his hand. "And what do you think about this?" He wiggles his wedding finger.

"Do we agree on this set then?" I ask him.

"Yes, I'll take this set." He looks over at Kaden, handing her his credit card.

Kaden gets the payment taken care of and walks back over with a ring sizer. "We need to be sure they fit nicely."

On the way home, I tell Jeremy it's good the cops are getting information from purchase receipts. "I would have never thought of it."

"That's their job, honey. They want to find Alicia as much as we do. Plus, I'm sure Alicia's mom is calling them every day to see if they have any updates."

"I'm just worried, it's been too many days, Jeremy. It's a week now. That's a long time not to return." I fiddle with the string on my sweater.

"Do you want to drive to the property we bought and see how the place looks now?" He locks our doors. "A distraction will be good for you."

I wonder if he's unsettled by it all too. "Sure," I say. "I'd love to see our place."

As we're driving and I see all the country areas, it puts me un at ease. Alicia could be anywhere. I know someone must have taken her because she'd never leave on her own accord. Alicia is a sweetheart. I can't imagine anybody ever wanting to hurt her. She doesn't have any enemies.

We pull up to the community gate, and Jeremy swipes the card. As it opens, my eyes wander around at all the beauty. I take in a deep breath then exhale slowly. We drive past the swim lake. It's still as blue as ever. It must be chlorinated. He drives up the hill on our property, and we park. I get out and say, "This is just what I needed."

Jeremy pulls his jacket tighter around him, "Me too."

"It'll be nice waking up to this view every morning. They keep it a park like setting. I love how they keep the grass cut and the weeds maintained."

Jeremy wraps his arm around me, "We all pitch in and pay a monthly fee for ground maintenance. It covers the swim lake being drained and cleaned every year too."

I ask, "How much is it?"

He answers, "Twenty-five a month."

I snuggle closer to him, "Wow, that's reasonable."

"Yeah, that's what I thought." He takes my hand. "Do you want to walk down to the river or sit on the dam?"

"Sure, let's go sit on the dam." We walk, but it feels more like we are hiking down the hill hand in hand. The whole time I have Alicia on my mind. This isn't fair. Maybe I could make some fliers. I'll call Sandy and see if she made them.

As we're sitting there, I let Jeremy know I keep thinking about Alicia. I ask him if he minds if I call Sandy now.

"No, not at all. I've been thinking about her a lot too." He looks out over the river.

"Sandy? This is Cassie."

"Oh, hi Cassie. I wasn't expecting to hear from you so soon. No new news yet."

I stand up to stretch my legs. I ask her, "I was wondering, did you make fliers?"

"I did and planned on putting them up this weekend. Would you like to help?"

"I certainly would. I'll see you this weekend, Sandy."

"Okay, bye Cassie."

She's the Prey, He's the Stalker

I fill Jeremy in on this weekend's plans. He tells me he'll go along and help as well. We're both staring off toward the river now.

Chapter 18

The backyard is done. Now all we need are the tables and BBQ pit relocated. The hag can't lift them, so it looks like I'll have to do that too. I go inside, and it's quiet. The kids are at school. I decide now is the time to tell her. "I want a divorce."

She looks at me horrified, "A divorce?"

I clarify myself, "Yes, a divorce."

"What about the kids? What about me? Did you meet someone?" She's crying now.

"We barely talk to each other. We live around one another, and that's no way to teach the kids what a relationship is all about. You can have the house, and I can see the kids on the weekends. As for me, I'll find an apartment somewhere."

"But I don't work... I quit when we couldn't afford the daycare costs. What am I supposed to do financially?"

I straighten my back and tell her, "You'll figure it out as time goes by, until then I will help with the expenses."

She throws a shirt at me, "Just get out! Go!"

I grab my keys and leave. I'll give her some time to think it over, hell, she may be happier in the long run. Where to go? I can drive past my dream gal's house again. See what she's up to. Hopefully, the man isn't there. I'm going to have to do something about him. He's always in our way.

He is there. I can't get too close because there's nothing but acreage of trees surrounding them. That's it. I'm going to have to think up a plan to dispose of him. I get back in my car, and as I'm driving to a local motel, I start conceiving ideas that'll take him out of the picture. Too bad I couldn't have hidden in the tree line again and waited for her to come out to play with the dogs. Nasty scoundrel. Always in the way.

I make my way to the motel. As I walk in, I notice it's nice compared to a lot of other places I've stayed. I'm not going to show up for work tomorrow. They'll be happy I did some house calls. I slip off my shoes and think of ways I can meet with the intruder of a spectacle. I have a home phone number and a recommendation by Rose, but what if she answers? I'll have to think of another plan.

The next day, I follow him, until he turns on a small backroad. I keep going, then I turn my car around to follow him. I go down a beautiful black top road, but the problem is I reach a gate. It looks like it takes a code. I back up and turn around. I could park here and walk inside and browse. I wonder if it would be too conspicuous. I could park up at the top of the hill and patiently wait for him to leave. I debate it, but I realize he'll probably go back to her place. It would hurt to know she's cheating on me again. I'm better off to not know. I drive back to the motel.

I sit on the bed and call the wife, "I need my clothes. I have to work tomorrow."

She says in a tone I'm used to, "All of your stuff is in the front yard."

I roll my eyes, "It's childish, but I'll come by and get my things in a little bit." I hope it doesn't rain.

I take a quick nap, and by the time I wake up, I realize I slept half the day away. I run my fingers through my hair, while looking at my reflection through the mirror. I splash some water on my face and head out the door.

When I get to the house, I grab all my stuff. She even had my laptop sitting on the porch. At least she put it in its case, and didn't throw it in the yard with the rest of my things. I open the trunk of my car and start loading stuff in. I can see her glancing at me through the window. I try not to look, though. I'm not in the mood for confrontation.

Once I have my stuff I drive off. I could hire my dream gal to show me rentals, but I'm not sure that would be a good idea. Instead, I grab the local paper from the gas station. I head back to the motel and unfold the newspaper on the desk. I unload the car first, then come inside, taking off my blazer. As I'm sitting at the desk going through the rentals, one catches my eye. It's above the coffee brewery. It's a four bedroom, which is what I need with the kids possibly staying on the weekends. Each will have their own bedroom. I immediately call and talk to the manager about filling out an application online, which she helps me with. It's just a waiting game now, to see if I get it. I don't know why I wouldn't. I'm a perfect tenant.

Next, I call up a divorce lawyer. I tell the secretary most of my information, and she sketches in an appointment for me tomorrow. I respond to her, "Thank you."

I feel I've achieved today's goals. I go back to the motel to unload all the things I collected from the yard. I put my laptop on the desk, clothes on the hanging rack, and shoes on the top shelf. That was easier than I thought it would be.

I'll have to follow him some more, to get an idea of how his schedule works and where would be the easiest place to confront him. The sooner the better.

Next thing I know, I'm opening my eyes. Shit, what time is it? I grab my phone and see it's 9 am in the morning. I quickly get up, slip on my shoes, and grab my jacket. I have every intention on following him this morning. I make some motel coffee, and I'm out the door.

Good, I see his car is still there. I park a little down the road in the direction they usually don't take. I sit there for a while but start to get restless. I'm not sure if it's the coffee or morning energy. Either way, I hope he comes out soon. He doesn't, but she does. She looks beautiful. She is wearing a blue, spring dress with a brown sweater.

Soon, he comes out too, but he gets in her car. Feeling

confused, I follow them. They lead me straight to the jewelry store. The same one I picked Alicia up from. What are they doing there? Maybe inquiring on her whereabouts? This is starting to get dangerously close. It's probably that douche she is with. I really need to do something about him and fast!

I take note that there's a café across the street. I park in the front and enter it. I'm starving. Some bacon and eggs could help with the bad mood I'm in. I take a seat on a stool at a counter. It's facing toward the window that looks directly at the jewelry shop.

A waitress with a name tag, Sally, walks up to me. "Can I take your order, Mister?"

I smile and wink at her, "Sure can. I'll take the breakfast boy platter."

She smacks her gum, pulls a pen out of her hair bun, and jots it down. I feel like I'm in the 1950s. The only thing missing is her in a poodle skirt. I stare back out the window when I notice Cassie's leaving the jewelry shop with him. I decide there's no reason to follow them anymore, since they're together. I need him alone. Maybe this weekend I can take care of it.

Chapter 19

The week passed somewhat quickly. Jeremy and I are getting ready to meet up with Alicia's mom, Sandy, to pass out fliers. "Honey, where did you put my razor blades?"

From the bedroom, I yell into the bathroom, "Third drawer on the right."

I slip on my sandals and go into the kitchen to make some coffee. I grab two cups and set them on the counter, next to the pot. I walk into the living room and turn the television on. I flip through, until I find the news. I then go back into the kitchen, and I pour Jeremy and myself a cup of coffee. I take it into the bedroom. Jeremy is putting on his sneakers. "Here's a cup of coffee for you babe."

"The liquid of the Gods," Jeremy says, with a halfcocked smile.

I sit on the end of the bed next to him. "I'm still not hearing any news about Alicia on TV. You'd think it would be all over it."

"Maybe it's not public knowledge because they don't want interference with the investigation."

I nod my head, "Yeah, that makes sense." I stand up, "Are you ready?" I look at my watch. "We're supposed to be there in like fifteen minutes."

He grabs his sweater, "I'm ready, babe."

The drive there was quiet and fast. Sandy was parked in the center of town. She went to the left to hang fliers and hand them out, and we went to the right. I ask Jeremy, "Do you think we should split up?"

"Come on, Cass. I want to spend some time with you." He hands me the handful of fliers. "You show me where, and I'll hammer and nail them up."

"I love you, Jeremy." I smile to myself more than to him. I like that he enjoys spending time with me. It makes me feel good.

I see a crowd of teenagers walking by me, and I hand a few of them fliers. "Have you seen this woman?" They mostly shake their heads or ignore me. "Okay, thanks." I guide Jeremy over to the electric post. "This seems to be a clear, view shot. Let's hang a poster here."

The flier has an oversized photo of Alicia, and at the bottom there's a phone number the person that recognizes her can contact. It also has the police contact information. It describes the last place she was seen and when. Her mom used hearts to border it. I feel a deep ache in my chest. "This is so sad."

"Are you getting hungry? We could invite Sandy to eat with us. There's a diner just down the street." Jeremy hangs another flier on a post.

"I could use the break." It's been about an hour since we started hanging the posters.

I follow Jeremy to where Sandy is, and he asks her, "Would you like to join us for an early dinner?"

Sandy walks to her car and opens the door, putting the tape and posters on the passenger side seat. "I've been having problems eating all week. I'm starting to feel weak. I think having dinner with you will be good for me."

Jeremy pulls me to the side and whispers, "I think it would be best if we don't talk about Alicia. Maybe give her a break unless she mentions her first."

I put my arm around his neck and give him a kiss on his cheek, "Agreed."

We get to the diner and sit at a circular, oak table. The waitress asks us for our drink order, and then we all look over the menu. Sandy says, "I know it's dinner time but breakfast sounds so good.”

“I was eyeing the omelet myself,” I nudge Jeremy. “What are you going to eat?”

He answers, “Steak and eggs are looking good to me. The menu says they serve breakfast all day, so we’re in luck!”

We make small talk while waiting for our food when Sandy says, “Oh, who am I kidding! I miss Alicia so much. She should be here eating with us. I just don’t understand.”

I tell her, “We went to the jewelry shop to look at rings the other day. I talked with Kaden. You’re familiar with her, right?”

Sandy answers, “We talked a few times.”

I continue, “She said the police had been in, and they were gathering receipts from the last few days Alicia was seen.”

“Oh, hon. That makes me feel better knowing they’re doing something. I feel so helpless. Most of the time I feel like I’m just sitting there while Alicia is in trouble. I hate that feeling.”

“I take it the police have been to her apartment?” I take a sip of my coffee.

“Yes, nothing out of sorts there. I can’t believe this is happening.” Sandy looks to me, and then looks to Jeremy.

He responds, “Neither can we.”

Once our food arrives, Sandy mainly picks at hers with her fork. I can’t even imagine what she must be going through. To have a daughter disappear with no signs left behind to give us clues where she went or who she is with. It must be terrible. I’m feeling lousy, and she was my best friend. I hadn’t spoken to her in months.

I look up, “Sandy, have you spoken with Rose?”

She answers, “Yes, she had no idea of her whereabouts either.”

“Are there any other friends she may have reached out to?”

“Just Kaden, who she works with, and we got all the

information from her that we possibly can."

I quiet down with the questions after getting a look from Jeremy. I guess she probably has taken all she can this morning.

Jeremy says, "I heard it's supposed to be nice weather this week. All sun, and no clouds to be seen in the sky."

It's pretty obvious he's trying to change the subject, but Sandy goes along with it. "Yes, maybe I can get some gardening done."

I say, "I haven't gardened since we adopted our third dog. They had him at a puppy mill that was shut down. He was so used to being in a cage that it took him awhile to warm up to the house."

Jeremy adds in, "And he wasn't used to people."

"Oh, that is just so sad." Sandy reaches for her water. "I'm glad he has a good home now. How old is he?"

Jeremy answers, "He's seven months."

I look over to Sandy, "We've had him since he was four months. He's really come a long way."

It's an hour later, and we've finished our dinner. "Do you want us to hang more fliers, Sandy?" Jeremy asks.

"No, hon. Thanks! I believe we've done all we can do for the day, and I'm feeling tired. I could use some sleep." Sandy responds.

I give her a hug. I ask, "How about you come over to our house tomorrow for lunch?"

"I'm sorry dear, I've made other plans with Susan. We're going to the local businesses to see if they'll hang fliers up."

Jeremy says, "Well, I'd normally say it was good to see you, but under the circumstances it is certainly not appropriate.

Chapter 20

By the time we get home, I'm pretty wiped out. After I let the dogs out, I'm ready to lie on the couch with Jeremy and snuggle, as we watch a movie. I get two wine glasses out and grab a bottle of sweet wine. I bring them into the living room, and then get the cover ready. "Jeremy, honey, what kind of movie are you in the mood for?"

"How about a drama. We did action last week." Jeremy comes in barefooted. "Or we could do a cookie cutter Hallmark movie."

"I'd rather do the drama." I look through the guide. I stop at a movie called, Misled. "This looks good. It's about a man that meets a woman on an online dating site. He's led to believe she's everything that she's really not."

Jeremy thumps down next to me, "Okay, it's triggered my interest. Let's watch it."

I hit play, and then I cozy in under Jeremy's arm.

I fell asleep halfway through the movie, which makes me feel bad. Jeremy is still sleeping. The dogs were in the yard the whole time, and it sprinkled. Now, I have dog paws tracked all through our house. I grab the mop and start cleaning up their mess.

Jeremy walks in a few minutes later and laughs. "Just imagine when there's a baby crawling all over the tracks."

"No Jeremy, I don't even want to imagine." I tiredly finish mopping. "Can you make us some coffee?? Pretty please?"

"Do you think our couch days will be over after we have a baby?" He asks me.

"I have a feeling they'll have just begun." I put the mop away and pour me a cup. "We just have to make sure we don't fall asleep with the baby in our arms on the couch. That would be a bad thing."

He says, "Did you know they're starting parenting classes at the Recklein? Sherri was telling me about it. You know she's six months pregnant now?"

I answer, "Where does time go? Does she know what the gender is?"

"A boy. She wanted me to tell you, she knows it's kind of late, but she's having a baby shower next weekend. She said you're more than welcome to attend."

I get in my purse and open my schedule binder. "I'm meeting with Molly Anderson Friday. What day is it on?"

He responds, "Saturday."

"Yeah, I can go. I have nothing on Saturday or Sunday."

He grabs my waist, "Oh, you need to fill me in on Sunday. That's our day."

I grab a pen and jot down, Jeremy, on Sunday's box. "There, all done." I hold the binder up and show it to him.

His smile stretches ear to ear, "Yes, I'm satisfied now."

I lean into him and give him a kiss. "I love you so much." I fully take in Jeremy, from his hair down to his cute bare toes.

He responds, "I love you so much too!" He wraps his arms around me. "I better go get dressed. I have to be at the Cedar place in less than an hour."

"Soon, you'll be passing by it on the way to our house." I wrap my arms around him, squeezing him tightly.

"River Hill the land of luxury." Jeremy puts his empty coffee cup in the sink. "I can definitely see myself kicking up my feet on the coffee table, looking out, and enjoying the river scene. I'm ready for it."

Jeremy leaves me in the kitchen by myself, while he gets ready for work. I call the three dogs in for breakfast. "There you go boys."

He calls out to me, "Have you seen my watch?"

I yell back, "You left it on the end table in the living room this morning."

"Oh yeah, that's right." He walks in and playfully thumps his forehead with his palm.

"Have a good day at work, babe."

He kisses my forehead, "I will. Are you home today?"

"Yep, just me and the dogs awaiting your arrival back."

He says, "It's hard to leave when you put it like that."

The dogs and I stand at the front door, watching Jeremy drive away. "Well, this is kind of depressing. You guys want to sit on the sofa with me and watch a movie?" They wag their tails and follow me from the door to the kitchen. "How about I pop us some popcorn first?"

The day goes by fairly fast. I finished the movie. The dogs are sleeping, and Jeremy is due back in an hour or so. My phone rings. I look around for it and find it on the kitchen shelf, next to the sink. "Hello?"

The other female voice says, "Is this Mrs. Jennings?"

I answer, "Yes."

She clears her throat, "I'm sorry to inform you, but your husband Mr. Jennings has been in a car wreck. He's in St. Jo's Hospital."

"Oh my God! Is he alright?"

"I'm not allowed to give any information over the phone, Mrs. Jennings. I was only told to call you and relay the message."

"Okay, okay, um, I'll be there in a minute." I quickly hang up the phone and slip on my shoes. I feel frantic, but I quietly leave to keep the dogs asleep.

Chapter 21

When I open my eyes, I'm in a hospital room. My entire body hurts, but I enjoy the pain. It reminds me I'm still alive. Everything but my head feels fine. I wonder if that man is dead. I intentionally rammed my vehicle into his. Maybe now I've ridden myself of the nuisance. Of course, they will never know I intended it to happen. They will see it as an accident. In fact, I'm going to blame him and say he ran a stop light. If he's breathing, it will be his word against mine.

One nurse walks in and checks my vitals. I tell her, "I need to make a phone call."

"You're awake!" She walks out and talks to another nurse. They both come walking in.

They do a full check on me. I say again, "Please, I'd like to make a phone call."

"I think it would be to your best interest to wait until the doctor talks to you."

I get quiet in my persistency, realizing she's right. Besides, maybe it's best I don't call the wife. I'm not sure I can handle the headache of her being here right now. With all that's going on, I think a rest will do me good.

"Hi, I'm Dr. Remeke. Everything looks fine, but we'd like to do a CT scan. You have a pretty nasty bump on your forehead. We'd like to be sure everything is fine before we send you home."

"When can I get the CT scan done?"

"As soon as we are through talking. Once I get the results back, if everything looks good, we can release you."

I use my remote to sit the bed up more. "Doctor, what happened to the other man?"

"He broke a few ribs, and he's still unconscious. We're not sure of the extent of his injuries yet. That's all the information I can give you. In fact, I probably said too much."

Damn, he's not dead. At least he's unconscious, and the doctor did say they don't know the full extent of his injuries. Maybe he will never wake up. Now that I have him out of the way, I can start concentrating more on the love of my life. I'm moved out, the divorce is in process, I signed up for a possible lease, and the man that keeps drooling over my woman is out of the way. Not too bad for a few days' work.

Soon, a male nurse pushes in a wheelchair and puts me in it. As we are wheeling through the halls I ask him, "Do you ever get tired of seeing sick and injured people?"

He responds, "Nope. I enjoy helping people."

After the CT scan he wheels me back to the room. I patiently wait around, while the doctor goes over my results. What feels like two hours have passed, when he finally comes walking in.

He says, "Well, Mr. Wilson, from the CT scan it looks like we see a tumor growth. We won't know a lot about it, until we run more tests. We will find out if it's benign. If it's malignant we will want to start treatment right away!"

Chapter 22

I come running into the hospital, frantic as hell. "Where is he? Where is my boyfriend? Jeremy Donahue?"

The nurse behind the information desk says, "Please, ma'am, slow down. Take a deep breath. Who?"

I answer, "Jeremy Donahue?"

She looks down at her keyboard and types in his name. Then she guides me to him. "He hasn't woken up yet. The doctor will be in briefly." She leaves me alone in the room, and I suddenly feel as if I'm going to have a panic attack when I look at Jeremy. He looks so helpless.

I take his hand in mine, and I whisper, "I love you." I kiss his forehead. "Wake up, baby." I squeeze his fingers. "Come on Jeremy, wake up." He doesn't even flinch. I massage his legs. Then I watch some television.

I look at the wall clock and realize it's already been two hours. I'm thirsty and decide to go to the cafeteria for some coffee. I hate leaving him. What if he wakes up and I'm gone? I whisper to him, "I'm going downstairs for some coffee. I'll be back soon." I study, watching for his eyes to flutter, anything that would be a sign of him hearing me. Nothing! I give him another kiss on his forehead.

The cafeteria is rather large. When you first walk in, it is shelves of pocket foods. To the left, is a fountain soda set up. To the right, is a line of people ordering what they want to eat. I didn't think about it being lunch time and the rush of doctors, nurses, and visitors who must be hungry.

I walk to the coffee brew section. I pick a large Styrofoam

cup and pour me some. My first sip is calming me, as I still feel the deep ache in my chest. It's weighing down each step I take. As I'm going back to his room, I pass a gift shop and decide to go in to browse. I find a plant I like and haul it back to his room.

When I walk in, there's a doctor there. "You must be Ms. Jennings." He holds out his hand. "I'm Dr. Remeke."

I put the plant on a nearby shelf and shake his hand. "Is there any information you can give me? Why is he still unconscious?"

Dr. Remeke says, "He hit his head pretty hard. According to the CT scan, he appears to have jarred his brain inside of the skull. It is hard to tell the extent of the damage, until we can run more tests. It will also be a great help to have you here when Mr. Donahue wakes up."

My hands are trembling, "Do you have any idea when he will wake?"

"It could be any time, or it could be a few days. I do not really have any more information for you, Mrs. Jennings." The doctor leaves the room, and I'm suddenly feeling all alone again.

I call Jeremy's parents, his brother, and my parents. I let them all know what the doctor said. His dad and mom are on their way, and later my parents will be joining us here at the hospital. My parents are flying back from Tahiti. I was surprised they weren't out and about in their RV.

"The plant makes the room feel cozier, Jeremy." I massage his thigh. "I think you'll like it."

Another two hours pass. I'm walking back in with another coffee. I see his parents making their way to his room. "Hi." I hug Mr. and Mrs. Donahue. "The doctor said they don't have too much information right now, but his brain has been jarred. They really won't know the extent of the damage until they do more tests, and he wakes up."

Mrs. Donahue says, "That sounds just awful. Just awful I tell you." She wipes away a tear.

We're all surrounding his bed now. Mrs. Donahue takes his hand, "Oh son, please wake up. I'm so worried." Mr. Donahue rests his hand on her shoulder and leans in to kiss her cheek.

She looks over at me and says, "Dear, while we are here why don't you go home and take a nap!"

"Well, I know I can't sleep, but I do need to let my dogs out and call Rose to see if she can take care of them while I'm staying at the hospital. I can also bring a change of clothes and stay the night." I take a deep breath, then continue, "And, um, I forgot what I was going to say."

Mr. Donahue says, "It's okay. I think we are all a bit lost."

On my way home, I call Rose, and set everything up. I'm lucky she's one of my best friends. I'm feeling really weighed down. I mean, first my best friend Alicia goes missing, and now the love of my life is in the hospital AND not waking up! It's just too much. I remember to also call about the baby shower and let them know I have to cancel, that my Jeremy is in the hospital.

When I finally arrive, the dogs are so happy to see me. They've been stuck in the house all day. I give them fresh water and feed them. While they're outside snooping around, I quickly grab my duffel bag and put a change of clothes in it. I decide a shower will do me good.

I quickly text Mrs. Donahue. "Is he awake yet?"

<h1 style="text-align:center">Chapter 23</h1>

I didn't sleep very well in the hospital room. I was in a laid-back recliner, but I couldn't get Jeremy off my mind. I kept thinking he'd wake during the night, or something might go wrong. As soon as I opened my eyes the next morning, I veered to his direction. He's still not awake.

Mr. and Mrs. Donahue went home last night. Mrs. Donahue tried to stay, but Mr. Donahue talked her out of it. He mentioned it's bad for her health at her age. He thought a good night's sleep would do her good, and that he'd drive her back this morning. I don't think they're here yet.

I stand up and stretch, then walk over to Jeremy. "Please, wake up, babe." I squeeze his hand and kiss his forehead. "Good morning." There's still no movement from him. "I'm going downstairs to get me a coffee, then I'll be right back." I talk to him just in case he can hear me.

The cafeteria is desolate. It makes it easier for me to get in and out. I look at my watch. Ten o'clock! No wonder! I grab my coffee and pay. Then, I head back upstairs. Through the elevator ride, a few tears fell. It's nothing I couldn't wipe away, as I quickly try to pull myself together. I see Mrs. Donahue. "Good morning."

She pats my shoulder, "Good morning, dear. How did you sleep last night?"

"The best I could. It's hard to sleep knowing that Jeremy could wake up at any given moment." We both walk back to the hospital room and look in on him.

Mrs. Donahue goes to one side of the bed, and I go to the

other side. She grabs his hand and says, "Jeremy, I am here."

His lips move, and we both stand in awe, looking to one another making sure we both saw it. I call out, "Jeremy, Jeremy?" His head moves to the left, and then to the right.

His mother says, "Jeremy, wake up. It's time to wake up now." His eyes open fast, then shut again.

I run out to the hall... "Nurse, doctor! Jeremy is waking up! Please, hurry!" A nurse quickly follows behind me.

She checks his IV. "Jeremy, are you awake?" His eyes slowly open.

I can tell right away something isn't right. It's as if his eyes are empty. His mom gives him a hug to the best of her ability. He just lies there like he's frozen. His body is stiff, and his lips are curved and tightly sealed. "Jeremy?" I take his hand in mine. "Are you okay?"'

The nurse says, "This may be too much stimulation for him right now. Can I ask you to step out, until the doctor gives him a quick exam?"

I look to his mother, and she is nodding at the nurse. Her face has worry all over it. I try to remain cool, calm, and collected. Once we are in the hall, I ask her, "Do you want a coffee? The doctor's not even on the floor yet, and it's going to take him a bit for the exam." I reassure her we have enough time. She takes my arm, and we head downstairs for the coffee.

By the time we get back upstairs, the doctor is there. We walk in, not sure if we're supposed to be in there or not. I take a seat at the window bench, and Mrs. Donahue stands on the other side of Jeremy. He's wide awake now. The doctor looks at us and says, "The head trauma has caused Jeremy to lose his memory. He is experiencing amnesia. He doesn't know who you are."

An hour later, and I'm grappling with an explanation I can hardly understand. His memory could be gone a day, or it could be gone a week. Dr. Remeke thinks it'll be short term, though.

I walk over to him, "Hi, Jeremy. I'm your fiancé." I grab his hand and kiss it.

He looks at me blankly, as if I'm a stranger. He says, "Hi."

Chapter 24

I'm back in the motel. I'm getting ready to celebrate getting the apartment. It gives me a nice place to go with my kids, and of course, once the man is gone, the love of my life will have a great kitchen to cook in. She's really going to like it. I can see her real estate office from the living room window. It'll be convenient for her to get back and forth to work by foot. My kids can go to the local stores and check out what's inside. Oh shit! Speaking of kids, how will they handle a new love being in my life? I guess in time they'll adjust.

Tomorrow, after doing a few signatures, I pick up the keys. It comes furnished, so I don't have to worry about doing much shopping. I just need to get bedding, dishes, and stuff like that. I wonder if I should wait for Cassie to help me with that.

I finish putting on my last shoe, tie it, and I'm out the door. I cross the street and enter the local tavern. I sit at the bar and order a draft Budweiser. There are a few people here, but it's not overly crowded. I'm looking up at the television, when a shaggy, red head sits next to me. She smells of too much perfume and bubble gum. She says, "Hey, handsome."

I quickly reply, "I'm married." No way would I ruin things with a woman like Cassie for this two-bit slut. I was never the cheating kind, and even if I were, it wouldn't be with her.

She twirls her hair in her finger, "Marriage ain't nothing but unhappiness." She smacks her gum, and I start feeling annoyed.

I look toward the bartender, as if pleading for help. He's too busy pouring a drink to notice. I grab her hand hard, "Look, I said I'm married. I'm not interested in a conversation with you."

She cries out, "Ow! You don't have to hurt me, mister. I get it." She walks down to the other end of the bar and sits.

I look at my watch, wasting time. I wonder if I can have the kids this weekend. I'll have to talk to the hag. I'll give her some money too. She's still got a copy of my credit card, so I'll just deposit extra into the account.

A few beers later, and I'm getting antsy. The red head is even looking better. I see a couple guys playing pool and decide to put three quarters up for the next game. They look disturbed, but hey it happens. I go to the juke box and put in a few bucks, choosing some Hank Williams and Willie Nelson. By the time I'm finished, it's my turn to shoot pool.

I win a couple games and decide I have to get up early. I make my way back to the motel. I throw my coat on the recliner that's seated beside a small, walnut desk. I look at the time and see it's still early enough to call the wife. I get a recording and leave a message, "Hi, it's me. I was just calling to see if I could have the kids this weekend." I leave a number for her to call me back on, even though she should know it by heart. I take off my pants and lie down, wrapping the sheet and blanket tightly around me.

I open my eyes to the sun shining directly onto me. A beam of light shines through, as if to blind me. I squint, as I get out of bed. I go to the bathroom and take a quick shower. I decide since I'm signing the lease, a suit would be most appropriate. I'm beyond excited. This is the second big step. The first being the divorce.

I get to the building and park in front. I'm early, so I go to the coffee shop underneath it. It's the brewery I always see Cassie at. Sometimes it's on her day off, and sometimes it's during her lunch break. She'll be ecstatic.

I make my way inside, and I get a coffee with a shot of

espresso. The girl behind the counter is a bit flirty and more than happy to make it for me. She tries with small talk, but I walk away to the other end of the counter as I wait for my coffee. Cassie wouldn't appreciate this girl's flirtatious attitude.

After I get my coffee, I sit at a table. It's in front of an elongated window. I'm watching families walk by. Some are going to the neighboring shops, while others look like they're hurrying to work. When I look at my watch, I realize it's time to go upstairs. I happily take my coffee and feel the rush of excitement from getting a new apartment. Soon, I will have the keys.

Chapter 25

We are packing up the plant and Jeremy is getting dressed. He still has no recollection of who we are. It's weird. He even looks a little different. Like some evil creature has stolen my fiancé's body, and it reflects in his eyes. I know that sounds mean given that Jeremy is not evil, but it does feel like some Sci-Fi movie. Maybe when we get home he will start remembering.

I ask him, "Do you think you'll remember how to drive?"

He shrugs, "I'm not sure."

I have to admit, he looks scared. Jeremy and scared are two things I've never seen together. As vulnerable as he is, is as confused as I am. As we drive past the countryside, I ask him, "Does any of this look familiar to you?"

He rolls down his window and quietly answers, "no," as if he's afraid to disappoint me. He looks over to me and says, "It's so weird. No matter how much I try to think back, all I get is a black, empty scene. There's so much I don't know about myself."

I tell him, "Once we get the dogs settled down, we can have a glass of wine, and I'll talk you through it. I'll give you a brief of who you were, are... Oh, hell, I'm not sure how to word it."

He smiles for the first time, "It's okay. I'm not sure how to word anything right now either."

His smile fills my whole body with relief. I continue to drive, until we reach our home. "Does any of this bring back anything?"

He gets out of the car and looks around, "I wish I could say it does."

I can hear the dogs barking inside. Rose steps out. "Sorry, I didn't know you were on your way home."

I put my hand over my mouth, "Oh my gosh, Rose. I'm sorry, I didn't call you. Everything just happened so fast."

She walks to her car, "They went out to do their potty time, they ate, and they've been loved on." She continues, "I have to leave in a rush. I have an appointment today. Love you."

I look over at Jeremy, who seems to be concentrating hard on trying to remember who Rose is. I tell her, "I love you too."

Jeremy holds the door open, so I can bring the plant inside. I look around for a good place for it and decide on the end table by the window. I pet the dogs, who are sniffing Jeremy. "He didn't cheat on you boys. He's been dog free." We both laugh.

"Do you want a glass of wine, Jeremy?"

"It certainly couldn't do anymore harm. Sure."

As I pour our glasses, I wonder if looking through photo albums might help him. If not, at least he'll be able to play a bit of catch up, to see how we got here. I wonder if he remembers anything about the accident. I do not dare ask about that yet. It's difficult because I have so many questions. "Are you hungry?"

He takes a glass and sits on the recliner, "No."

I go to the bookshelf and pull down three thick photo albums. I sit two of them on the coffee table, then pat the seat next to me. He relocates, and I open the first page.

We go through the wine and albums in a couple hours. The dogs are getting as restless as my legs are feeling. "I better let them out."

He follows us to the backyard and says, "So I'm an architect?"

I look to the ground and smile, "Yes."

He looks rather proud. "Do I work tomorrow? How am I supposed to know what I'm doing?"

"No, I called in for you and explained the car wreck. I mean, eventually you'll have to go back, but let's not worry about that right now."

He gets quiet, which worries me. He then takes one of the dogs' balls and throws it across the yard. "Get it, boy. Fetch."

By the time night falls, I'm completely drained and worn out. Jeremy asks, "Do you mind if I sleep on the couch until I start feeling comfortable?"

I'm taken by surprise. "Sure," I answer. I go to the closet and pull out a comforter for him to use. I take his pillow from the bed, and I make the couch up for him.

He says, "Thanks. This must be weird for you."

As I walk back to the bedroom I say, "It's just as weird for you."

I toss and turn most of the night. I don't have Jeremy to snuggle up to, and what if he's stuck like this for long term? Will we be happy? So many questions are running through my mind. I give up and get up. I tiptoe toward the kitchen. I want to make some warm cocoa. I'm hoping it will help me sleep. As I pass Jeremy, I sneak a peek of him sleeping soundly.

I must have been too loud in the kitchen because he walks in. "Do you have enough for two?"

"Oh, I didn't mean to wake you!" I stir in the cocoa. I add a few marshmallows from the jar my mother gave me five years ago.

He hands me a cup from the cabinet, "To be honest, I wasn't sleeping too good. I keep trying to remember. It's kind of terrifying to not be sure of anything or anyone. It's like waking up to a world of strangers. I tested myself to see if I could read. Which I could! Thank God!"

I hadn't even thought of that. It's like having to learn most things all over again. I say, "Maybe a good night's sleep will help jolt your memory."

We both enjoy about an hour of conversation. As we walk back in, I ask, "Would you like to sleep on the bed, and I could sleep on the couch?"

"No way. This is the most comfortable couch I've ever laid on."

I laugh and ask, "And how would you know? You wouldn't remember to compare."

Chapter 26

The night was hectic, but the morning with Jeremy was beautiful. We sat on the front porch swing, talking about how we met, how we were so in love, and the plans we made. Today, I'm taking him to the property we bought that we're building a house on. It's almost finished. Without Jeremy's memory, we can't add the final touches on it. I'm patiently waiting.

On the drive there, I tell him we planned on getting married on the property and having babies. He seemed as overwhelmed as I usually look when Jeremy talked to me about it. It seems strange being in the other shoes. I make a mental note to be a bit more optimistic when he discusses marriage and babies to me.

We drive down the country road. Summer has taken place, so the trees are in full bloom. Jeremy looks around anxiously. "This is breathtaking."

"You haven't seen anything yet." I open the electronic gate with my card.

As we pass by the swimming lake, Jeremy says, "Wow, do you use that?"

"We haven't had the opportunity yet. We aren't moved in. You have to live here or be a guest in order to use it. Second thought, we probably could, being that we're building on the property, but we never have."

He rolls down his window and says, "If this was my place, I'd be jumping in."

I look over at him in wonder. Then I say, "Jeremy, this is

your place."

He says, "Oh, right, right." He then gets real quiet for a few minutes.

I try to break the ice, "Wait until you see the view from the porch and inside windows." I pull up the hill's driveway.

We get out of the car, and Jeremy looks around. "This is like a dream."

"It is a dream. It's our dream." I take the keys out, and as I'm getting ready to unlock the front door, it opens.

A construction worker says, "Hi, I'm Bob. My crew and I were just leaving."

I take Jeremy inside, and he's standing in awe. "This is great! It's manly, but with a woman's touch. Not too feminine for my taste." He laughs, "Whatever my taste is."

I give him a tour. "So, none of this looks familiar to you?"

He simply answers, "No. I sure do love all the wood."

I explain to him, "It's almost finished. It just needs the final touches on it. I can't do it until you gain back your memory."

"Well, technically, we could. I just don't know if I'd agree with myself. Weird huh?"

I answer, "Very."

"Being here with you makes me sad considering the state you're in. Let's head back, we'll stop at the grocery store, and I'll make dinner."

He follows my lead, "Sounds good to me."

It's bizarre. He's bizarre. He looks exactly like Jeremy, talks like Jeremy, but has no recollection of our past together. Also, at times it's as if his eyes develop an emptiness. I miss Jeremy, even though he's right next to me. We're probably spending more time together than we ever did, but it's like he's not really here.

We get to the grocery store, and as we pass some food aisles, I accidentally bump into a man. He says, "Hi, I'm Albert Wilson. I'm not sure if you know me or not, but I was in the other vehicle in the accident with your husband."

I grab his sleeve, "Albert, could you please tell us what happened?"

Albert says, "Your husband ran a stop sign. I understand how things like this can happen. I'm not filing any charges against him. Did he have any serious injuries?"

"My fiancé is experiencing amnesia. He can't remember anything before or during the accident."

He extends out a hand, "I'm Jeremy, aka fiancé." As they shake, Jeremy continues, "I'm sorry about the stop sign. I'm not sure how that happened."

Albert picks up a box of crackers, "It happens. Accidents happen all the time. Now had you been drunk, I would have filed charges."

I feel relief in my shoulders, "Well, it was nice meeting you, Albert. I better get Jeremy home where he can get a good dinner and some sleep."

Albert looks at me with an intensity that sends chills up my arm, "It was my pleasure seeing you here, Cassie."

Once we get in the car, I look at Jeremy and ask, "How did he know my name?"

Jeremy responds, "Maybe you said your name when he introduced himself."

I think back, "Yeah, maybe."

Chapter 27

Oh, that was fun! Seeing Cassie and Jeremy wasn't even on my list of things to do today. Now I know his name, he has no memory, and I just got away with a crime. Fiancé? I don't like that. He's also still alive, which is not what I want. I'll have to think up another plan.

For now, I shall celebrate success. I have my new apartment, and the soon to be ex-wife said I can have the kids this weekend. I think I'll take them to Six Flags. They could use the break, and I need the laughter. Everything's been serious lately with the moving out, divorce, and the car wreck.

How can I get rid of Jeremy? Maybe with him having amnesia it will be easier. How can I get that to work for me? I'm going to have to do some serious thinking before this weekend, so I'm not wasting the whole time thinking about the jerk, while my kids are here. Why would she be marrying him? It must have been before she met me. I saw how she was rubbing her arm. I have no doubt that I gave her goosebumps. She doesn't remember me at all, and we've met a few times. I guess it's not really a wonder with everything she has going on and the daily clients she meets.

I look around the apartment and make a list of everything I need. I write down dishes, pots and pans, silverware, rags, dish towels, etc. The list keeps getting bigger. It reminds me that I have some coupons from Bed, Bath & Beyond.

I grab my jacket and head to the store. When I get there it's semi busy. As I'm walking through, I'm reminded of everything I forgot to put on my list, like bath towels. By the time I'm finished getting everything I need, my cart is full. I go to check out.

The ride home, which to still say feels strange, was easy. There wasn't any traffic. I dread carrying all of this up and the stairs. Yet, I know it will keep me busy and help pass the time. Also, I need to get it all done before Monday because I have to work. Since, I'll be busy with the kids this weekend, that leaves today.

It's my last load up, and I feel like my legs are going to give in. I make myself a tall glass of ice water. After a few gulps, I start unloading everything. Afterward, I decide I'll take a quick shower and change my clothes. I'm going to see what Cassie is up to today. Seeing her made me miss her more.

On the way to her house, a tractor gets in front of me. He's driving too slowly. I swerve to the side of him and pass. A car I hadn't seen because of a hill, almost hit me. It would have been a head on collision, but at the last minute, luckily, I was able to pass the tractor. My hands are still shaking. She's worth it.

I park down the street. I see her dogs are outside, but the car is gone. His vehicle is there, but I doubt he's driving right now. I wonder if he's home and if she's gone. I doubt it. I walk up to the front door and knock. Nobody answers. I take my credit card out, and mess with the doorknob. It was easier than I had expected.

I see how cozy her place is. I go up the stairs and find the bedroom. I look through her drawers and take out a pair of her panties. I quickly put it in my pocket and leave before they get home. As I'm coming down the stairs, I notice all the photos. I see one that must be her with her mom and dad. I study it for a second, before realizing I better get the hell out of here.

I'm glad to get back to the apartment. When I open the door, I'm amazed by how perfect for me it really is. Now that I have a blender and coffee maker on the counter, it adds character. I go into the bedrooms and put the kids twin sheets and comforters on their beds. By the time I'm finished, I'm exhausted. I take off my shoes and don't even bother with my clothes. I just fall onto the bed.

The next day is going by fast because I'm excited to get my three kids. My youngest son, Joey, is thirteen. He can be a handful at times, but he can also be the biggest heart of them all. My middle girl, Maggie, is fifteen. She's a hell raiser right now. She argues with her mom constantly, but she's crazy about me. We get along great. My eldest son, Randall, is seventeen. He is good. He's hardly ever home, and when he is, he's locked up in his bedroom with the music blaring. They're why I chose Six Flags. It's good for all ages.

I look at my watch and realize it's time to get them. I make the final touches on the apartment. I figured the boys could share a room, and Maggie will have her own. Soon, Randall will have an apartment of his own and won't need to stay over.

When I get to the house, my soon to be ex doesn't look happy to see me at all. Her face is all contorted inward, as if her face is deflating like a balloon losing helium. I ask, "Are the children ready?" She puts her hand on her hip and says, "I hope you have a place for them to stay now. The motel is creepy and nasty. Maggie definitely doesn't need to be there."

I hold my hand up, as if that will stop her from talking, "Alright already. I have an apartment now." I tell her, "It's above the coffee brewery." I know she knows where that's at because we've been there together on quite a few occasions.

The kids throw their bags into the trunk before getting in. I stare back at them, "Guess where I'm taking the lot of you?"

Joey looks all excited and says, "I don't know, Daddy, just tell us."

Randall punches Joey in the arm, "I can't believe you still call him Daddy."

Maggie whines, "Daaaaad, make them stop. They're

wrestling again."

"Okay kids, if you want to go to Six Flags you have to simmer down."

They get excited about Six Flags, and the car goes from total chaos to silence.

Chapter 28

Not much has changed with Jeremy. I feel like I'm losing my mind. My patience is running thin, and I'm really missing my old Jeremy. I get on the phone with Rose, "Hey girl, are you up for lunch? I really, really need someone to talk to."

"Sure, give me a bit to slip out of these sweats and into some jeans. I'll meet you at the Coffee Brewery in like 20 minutes?"

I let out a sigh of relief, "Sounds great, see you then."

I walk into the living room. Jeremy's sitting on the couch, watching 60 Minutes. "Jeremy, I'm going to meet my friend Rose for lunch. Do you want me to bring you something back?"

He says, "Nah, that's okay. I'll make a sandwich here."

During the drive to see Rose, I'm singing along, "Isn't it ironic? Isn't it, though?"

When I get in the coffee shop, I look around for Rose and find her sitting at a round table in the corner. I take off my long sleeve flannel and put it on the back of a chair. I give her a hug. "Oh my god, I'm going crazy, Rose."

She looks at me with concern, "What's the matter, Cassie?"

"So much has happened that I didn't have a chance to tell you. Jeremy got into a car wreck a few weeks ago."

"That's terrible, Cassie! Is he alright? Were you in the car with him?"

"No, I wasn't in the car. Jeremy's body is alright, but he's suffering from amnesia." I wipe away a tear. "I know this sounds selfish, but him not being himself is so frustrating. He sleeps on the couch every night now. He doesn't recognize anything, and he hasn't been back to work yet. It's like living with a stranger."

"I'm sorry you're going through all of that, Cassie. I can't even imagine how it must feel. I've never been around anyone with amnesia before." I can tell she feels bad that I'm crying, but she just sits there. Hugging me would only make things worse, and I think she knows that.

I tell her, "All of this stress on top of missing Alicia, it just feels like a lot."

Rose asks, "How did the accident happen?"

I hold my head in my hand and let out another sigh, "The other guy, Albert, said that Jeremy ran a stop sign and they collided."

"Agh, I didn't even ask if you want a coffee and something to eat?"

I ask her, "Did you order already?"

"Just this coffee, but I'm hungry."

We both get up and walk to the counter to order. I get a panini and she gets a bowl of soup. "I'll also take a large coffee and this bottle of water."

While I'm waiting for the girl to call out my name for the order, I tell Rose, "It's crazy living like this. The only thing keeping me sane is knowing that he will gain back his memory, eventually."

"It's bizarre, like not knowing when," Rose says, as she leans on the counter getting a closer look at an apple pastry. "Maybe I should have ordered that too." She points at it.

"Right. Is he going to wake up one night and ta-da, back to normal?"

The girl calls out, "Rose, Rose."

Rose takes her soup tray and says, "Meet you at the table."

I look impatiently at the girl who banters, "It's coming, it's coming."

Another girl calls out, "Cassie, Cassie."

I retrieve my food and make my way back to where Rose is sitting. I'm so busy staring ahead, I end up tripping right in front of everyone. I can feel my whole face go beat red, as the tray flies on the floor of the next table. The same girl I gave the disturbing look to comes to help me up. "Are you okay?" She asks, as she takes me by the arm.

"I'm fine, really. I'm not sure what I tripped on, but I'm okay."

She says, "Let me get you a new order. It was the panini, right?"

I want to hide under a rock. "Yes, a panini... the chips are still in the bag, so they'll be fine."

Once Rose sees I'm okay, she laughs and can barely say, "At least it wasn't..." She laughs some more... "It wasn't soup."

"Okay, smarty pants. You just wait. One day you'll get my age and question if getting up is even an option."

"Oh, Cassie you're like... three years older than me. You make it sound like you're ready for grand motherhood, and you're not even a mom yet."

"Rose, if he doesn't get his memory back, I'm not sure I'll ever be a mom."

Rose takes a drink of her Ginger Tea. "He'll get his memory back. How long has it been... you said like two weeks?"

I nod my head and say, "It feels like a lifetime already."

The girl brings my panini. I tell her, "Thank you."

She smiles at me. "Are you sure you're alright?"

I look down at the table and say, "I'm fine."

Rose says, "You do have a nasty bruise on your forehead."

I take out my makeup mirror and look. "Eww, that is nasty."

When we are finished with our food, I give Rose a hug goodbye. "Do you think you can join us for dinner tomorrow and see the new Jeremy for yourself? Maybe seeing you might jog his memory.”

Rose says, “Sure, let me ask Chris first, though. I’m sure he’d love to see Jeremy. They always did get along good.”

She texts Chris, while I put my flannel back on. She looks back up from her phone and says, “He said it sounds like a plan, Stan.”

I repeat, “Stan?!”

She shrugs, “It’s just his way.”

Chapter 29

"So, hon, I have to go to the grocery store to get steaks. Rose and Chris will be joining us. Does that sound okay with you?"

He enters the kitchen and sits at the breakfast counter. "Chris, Chris." I make him a glass of water and pass it to him. He takes a drink and then says, "Rose and Chris."

"Are you too tired? Maybe this is just too much for you."

He responds, "No, no. I think having them here is great! I'm sorry, I've been cooped up. I know this must not be easy for you."

"There you go thinking about me again. Let's concentrate on you. Maybe seeing Chris again will jog your memory. You two used to be good friends. Of course, we got busy in our life, planning the new house, marriage, and a baby." There's that look of his again. The overwhelmed one.

He says, "Yeah, I guess so. It's weird, I catch myself thinking... when I get my memory back will I still be me, or will it be like I'm someone else again?"

As I pour myself a cup of coffee, I explain to him, "I think it will feel natural." I put the pot back on the burner. "Would you like to go to the grocery store with me?"

"Sure, it'll do me good to be out and about. Give me about fifteen minutes to shower and change."

I finish off the last of my coffee, then call for my three dogs. "Come on, boys. Let's go out back." I take their ball and run around the yard. "Can't get me." They come chasing after me. A few minutes later and I'm on the ground.

They're licking my face.

Jeremy calls out, "Looks like they won." He comes toward me and holds out his hand. I grab it, laughing. He says, "Oh no, looks like you've bruised yourself."

"No, that's from earlier. Embarrassingly enough, this isn't the first time I've met the ground. Unfortunately, I tripped and fell yesterday, when having lunch with Rose."

"Wow, and this whole time I haven't noticed?"

"Well, to be fair. You slept a lot, and I've noticed that my bruise is getting darker by the hour."

I wipe the dirt off the back of my pants, and we end up holding hands inside to the house. He asks, "This was fun, yeah?"

"Yeah, it sure was. So, are you ready for the market?"

He holds out his arm to show me his muscles, "Yeah, I think I can take it on."

During the ride, a Bryan Adams song comes on, "It cuu-uuuuts like a knife ooOoo yeah but it feels so right." Of course, I'm singing along like crazy. What surprises me is Jeremy is singing it too. I say, "You remember the words?"

"Hey, I guess I do." He gets really quiet, then he starts singing again.

A few more songs later and we arrive to the parking lot. I'm looking for a place to park when a damn sedan backs right into my little Prius. Jeremy's eyes look like they're ready to pop out of his head. I ask him, "Are you okay?"

He rubs his eyes, "Sorry, just a bit of PTSD. It's almost as if my mind was trying to have a flashback. At least, momentarily... then nothing."

"No, that's great! It's trying Jeremy, and that's something."

A woman knocks on my window. "Are you guys okay in there? I didn't mean to back into you. I didn't see you. I have my insurance, and I've called the authorities. They should be here any minute."

By the time we're done trading insurance information

and talking to the police, it's been an hour. I look at Jeremy, "We're going to have to make this quick. I'll text Rose and let her know we're running late."

We get inside the grocery store and Jeremy is experiencing a bit of what is like Vertigo. I can't say for sure because he needs to go back to see the doctor. I dial the phone and make him an appointment. "It's okay, Jeremy. We can cancel Chris and Rose and just go home."

He says, "No, I really want to do this dinner. Besides, the new me hasn't tried your steak."

We get home, and I immediately start dinner. Jeremy is sweetly by my side, pulling lettuce for the salads. I ask him, "Can you put the wine in the fridge, so it's nice and chilled before they get here?"

"Sure can," he washes his hands and gets the wine.

Soon my doorbell is ringing, and there are Rose and Chris standing in the doorway. "Hey girl!" She gives me a hug.

Chris hands me a bottle of wine, "Something smells good."

I hand the wine to Jeremy. He puts it in the refrigerator. He looks at me, "Have I always drank wine?"

I nod my head yes, and I accidentally take him in for a hug. "I'm sorry if that made you uncomfortable. Old habits die hard."

"It's okay. I rather enjoyed it," he smiles at me, as he finishes the salads.

I ask Rose, "Do you mind if I let my dogs back in?"

Rose says, "Of course not."

I open the back door, and all three run to Chris and Rose. I yell out, "Favoritism."

Chris says, "That's a good boy." He's talking to Bandit, while Scamp licks Rose's cheek. Colombo Columbus is close to the stove now, smelling all the food.

"On second thought, I think I'll let them back out until after we are done eating... or they're bound to drive us crazy as we try to enjoy our meal." I offer them treats, and out they go.

Rose says, "They're all so cute."

Chris says, "I wish we could have a dog."

Rose adds in, "Our landlord won't let us, but we're saving up for a house, and then we can have one, Chris. Don't be so sad about it." She pats his back.

I dish the food onto the plates, while Jeremy tosses the salads, adding it in bowls. "Where do you plan on buying a house at?"

Chris says, "We aren't sure yet."

I set the plates on the table. "You should see the place where we're building a house. It's an old fishing resort campground. They've taken a lot of the cabins and renovated them. You should look into buying close to us."

"Oh, Chris doesn't that sound like fun!" Rose gets all excited.

Jeremy tells Chris, "That's not all. It has six huge lakes throughout the campground, one of which, is a swim hole. It has slides and pavilions with a fire pit. It's an absolute dream."

I look at Rose, "It also has a playground with a mini house for the kids. It has a tennis and basketball court." I take a quick breath and continue, "Most of the cabins there have a lake front view. Ours has a creek that runs through it too."

"Sounds heavenly," Rose says.

"Do you want me to get prices and listings. Don't forget if you want to build a house on a piece of property, that's something that can be done."

Chris says, "Sure. How far is it from town, though?"

I say, "It's out past 72. I'd give or take five to ten miles."

He replies, "That's not bad. Not bad at all. The more I hear about this place, the more I like it."

"How much are you wanting to spend?"

Chris answers, "About two hundred and twenty thousand."

"Oh, you can definitely get something there."

Rose says, "How fun!!!!"

When we're done eating, Chris comments how great the food was, and Rose is agreeing with him. We take our wines into the living room. "Anyone up for a board game of Scattergories?"

Chapter 30

"Agggghhhhh! I'm not sure my old self can take this."
The Thompson Rollercoaster is going left, right, and upside
down. I'm feeling dizzy as hell. I'm pretty sure my heart is
going to thump right out of my chest, or worse yet, come
right out of my mouth.

"Oh, come on Dad! This isn't even the scariest one. I'm
only twelve, and I'm not scared."

"Yeah Dad, Joey is right. You can do this," Maggie tries
to encourage me.

Randy adds his two cents in, "Suck it up old man. This
is life right before our very eyes." Of course, he would have
to be the deeper thought out one. I'm positive at any given
second I'm going to puke. Right when I can't stand it any
longer, it's over.

Joey asks, "Dad, can we get some cotton candy?"

"Food?! Food? How can you even think of food after that
non-joyride?"

Joey just laughs.

Randy says, "Actually, Dad, I am getting kind of hungry."

Maggie adds in, "Me too!"

I tell them, "There's lots to choose from. We can go to the
center of the park. They have a ton of booths set up with all
different food selections. Joey, you stay close to one of us,
though."

"Okay Dad, geez, but I'm not a baby anymore."

"I'm not saying you're a baby, but there's a lot going on.

I don't want any of us getting lost. We'll find a table first, that we can all meet at after."

It seems like it took us thirty minutes to find the center of the park. It's a big place. We all get to the booths we want, and Joey agreed with me on Chinese. He's standing right in front of me. "Do you want egg rolls with yours?"

He quietly and shyly says, "Yeah."

We all get to the table and sit down with our food. We talk about our week. How their mother is doing! Apparently, she's working for the jewelry company Alicia worked for. It really makes me feel uncomfortable. I try to get more information out of the kids, but there wasn't any more to learn. She started last week. They said she's happier than they've seen her in a long time. That kind of hurt my feelings, but I guess they're right. Our marriage had been dying out for years.

"Does your mom know where my apartment is?"

Randy answers, "You told us to tell her, so she could pick us up Sunday. Remember?"

"Oh yeah, that's right. As I age, my memory gets worse." I think about Jeremy and his memory loss, and I feel thrilled.

"Are you kids ready to go home?"

"Oh, come on, Dad. Let's at least do Thunder River first," Maggie exclaims.

"Fine, fine. A hot day like this, Thunder River will be great!"

The line is long, but the kids are worth the wait. It's a hot day, so cold water sounds good.

There's a stand for frozen lemonade as we wait. I get four, one for each of us.

Randy says, "We don't have to wait if you don't want to, Dad. The kids will be fine."

"No, no. I want to wait. I think it's a great way to end the day."

Thunder River was a hit with the kids. Joey and Maggie ended up underneath the waterfall and got soaked. They laughed and laughed. Joey fell asleep on the way home, and Maggie was singing. Randy had a big smile on his face, so I know I did good.

As I carry little Joey up the stairs, I wonder if Cassie would find this to be romantic. She really missed out on a good time with us, but there is plenty of time to do it again. I put Joey in bed and snuggle him in his covers. I tell Randy, "Goodnight."

Chapter 31

"I'm so excited to show the property to Rose and Chris today! We should have made a day of it and went swimming and roasted hot dogs. In fact, how does that sound to you if we do?"

Jeremy looks up from the newspaper, "I think it sounds like fun. Let's do it. Wait... do I own swim trunks?"

I laugh, "You sure do. I'll call Rose right away, let her know of our plans, and see if she agrees."

"Hey, Rose?"

She answers, "Yeah? You're not calling to cancel, are you?"

"No way. I'm calling to see if you want to make a day of it. We can go swimming, roast some hot dogs at the pavilion, and maybe do some s'mores?"

She calls out, "Hey Chris, want to do some swimming and roast some hot dogs?"

I can hear him call back out, "Sure."

She gets back on the phone and says, "Sounds good. Let's do it."

"Do you want to meet me at the grocery store?"

Rose asks, "What time?"

I respond, "How about in an hour?"

She mocks Chris, "Sounds like a plan, Stan."

The time goes by fast. Before we know it, it's time for us to leave. I almost forgot to grab the towels, but I remember at the last minute. I put them in my beach purse and grab my sun hat. "I'm ready, honey." It's still hard not to call him names like babe, honey, etc. I've noticed he never responds to me in any pet names.

He yells from the bedroom, "Putting on my last sandal now."

The drive there was quiet. Jeremy mainly looked at the scenery. It was okay because I just listened to music. I'm used to the scenic drive now. I guess everything is new through Jeremy's eyes.

When we get to the grocery store, I ask Jeremy, "Do you want to stay in the car or go in with me?"

"I'll go inside with you," he answers.

I see Rose and Chris pull up. "Hey guys, over here." I'm waving my arms in the air, to the point Jeremy laughs at me.

Chris walks over to Jeremy, "I'm only here for the s'mores."

Jeremy responds, "I'm here for the hot dogs."

Rose and I, both in unison say, "Swimming." Then we giggle.

We finish with grocery shopping, and I ask Rose, "Do you want to take one vehicle or two?"

She says, "We better take two, just in case we leave early."

We get to the road, and I keep watching behind me, in the rear-view mirror, to see Rose's reaction.

She looks mesmerized. That comes as no surprise to me, considering the rolling hills coming here, and then going down to the valley to be met by lakes. It's a beautiful combination. We get to the swim lake, and we park in the spots they have allocated for everyone. "Here we are," I smile at Rose.

"This is absolutely stunning, Cassie!" Rose looks over to Chris, "Couldn't you just imagine living here?"

"I'm taken with it. Can you get us a list of the houses for sale, Cass?"

I answer, "Sure can!"

It's a hot, sunny day. I grab my beach bag from the car,

take Jeremy's hand in mine, and we make our way to the pavilion. The two fountains are going in the lake, making it look even cooler. On a day like this, it's perfect! Rose and Chris are already in. I ask Jeremy, "Are you ready?"

His smile broadens, "I sure am."

I get in and splash Rose. She splashes me back. Then, the guys put us on their shoulders, and we fight with a few noodles that were left at the pool from the previous swimmers. I knock poor Rose so hard she falls into the water. She says, "Hey now, no fair!" We all end up laughing.

When we're finished swimming, we all dry off and prep the hot dogs and s'mores. "This is so much fun. I can imagine doing this all week." Rose shifts her weight to her left foot. "At least, like, three times a week."

Chris looks over at Jeremy, "We could start a poker night with the guys too."

"Yeah, that sounds good." Jeremy hands Chris a soda, then takes a seat at the picnic table under the pavilion. We all seem content and ready to relax now.

A few hours later, we are packing our things up. Rose says, "I really had fun, Cassie. Thanks for inviting us."

Chris adds, "Don't forget to get us the list of houses."

"I won't, and I'll work for the two of you for free."

Rose gives me a hug, "You're the best."

By the time Jeremy and I arrive home, we are wiped out. Swimming takes so much energy. I'm not sure what Jeremy likes to watch, but I ask him anyway, "Do you want to do some wine and television tonight?" I can't imagine he'd want to snuggle.

"Sure," he says. He goes into the bedroom to change his clothes first. I wait until he's done, and then I change mine. Really, we probably need a shower, but we're so tired neither of us do. Oh my gosh, to shower with my Jeremy, sounds heavenly. I miss him so much. He has a doctor appointment soon. It seems to be taking longer than Dr. Remeke had suspected. I decide to text Rose.

Me: Did Jeremy seem oddly strange to you? Or like the same old Jeremy?

I pour both of us a glass of blackberry wine. I carry them into the living room and hand Jeremy his. I take note that he's sitting on the recliner again. It's strange to sit on the couch alone in his company. I get him a throw cover and hand it to him. Then, I get mine from the desk chair. "What do you want to watch?"

"Totally up to you."

My phone dings, but I ignore it, as I flip through the channels. I see Crime Investigation. "How about this?"

He pulls the cover up to his chin, "Seems interesting." He says, "Is it just me or is it chilly?"

"It's chilly to me, after being in the sun all day. I have a bit of a burn on my upper chest and shoulders. I also notice your nose is red."

He rubs his nose, "Oh no, I'm Rudolph."

An hour later and I'm tired. I make my way, again alone, to the bedroom.

Chapter 32

The next day, I go into the office, finally. Marge says, "Look who finally made her way in."

I tell her, "I need listings for River Hill."

She asks, "Isn't that where Jeremy and you are building your house?"

I explain, "Yes, my friends, Chris and Rose, are wanting to buy a house in the same community. I told them I'd do it pro bono. They're very good friends of mine. They're basically like family."

She says, "I believe I've heard you talk about them before. Do you have any other listings right now?"

I look at her a little surprised by the question, "No, I closed on the other three. Oh, and the condo."

"The reason I ask you is, the Hughes are looking for a place, and they don't have a broker for it yet. Would you be interested? I know right now you have a lot going on with Jeremy. It's up to you if you're up for it."

I sit in front of the computer and type in River Hills. "Actually, anything to keep me busy right now is a good thing."

I check my phone and see Rose had texted me back.

Rose: He definitely doesn't seem like our Jeremy, but let's give him time. I can tell he's trying.

Me: Yeah, maybe you're right. Maybe I'm trying to rush things too fast. I just miss him so much.

I look up River Hills for properties in their price range and print up a sheet of listings. There are still plenty available because it's just been renovated recently into selling homes instead of leasing out cabins.

I look over at Marge's office to see if she's still there. Thankfully, she is. I walk in and ask her, "Do you have the Hughes information? I'll call them before leaving today."

She hands me a post-it note with their name and budget. "Do you know what area they're looking to move to?"

She says, "I haven't a clue."

I walk back to my desk and call them right away. "Hi, is this Mrs. Hughes?"

"Yes, may I ask who is calling?"

"This is Cassie. Cassie Jennings. I'd like to represent you in finding your dream home. Marge gave me your number and told me your budget. I need to know what area you're interested in."

"Oh, hi Cassie! It's nice hearing from you. Sure, we'd be pleased if you represent us. We are looking at the area of Marble Springs. Are you familiar at all with it?"

I hold the phone with my shoulder and ear, while typing in Marble Springs. "I sure am. I'm pulling listings on it now. Would you like to see some this evening or is that not enough notice?"

"Let me check with Mr. Hughes, and I will get back to you as soon as he answers."

"Okay, it was a pleasure talking with you, Mrs. Hughes."

I stick around the office for a couple more hours to look up listings within their price range for the Marble Springs area. Soon, she calls me back to let me know this evening will be fine. I also pulled up a few more listings that just came on the market yesterday, for Chris and Rose. I text her:

Me: When do you want to go and see these houses? Does Tuesday work for you, or is Chris working?

I put my phone down and look up Marble Springs, to be sure I printed up all I can find within their price range.

This community has amenities of its own. It's an expensive area. Most of the houses are on a golf course. It has a swimming pool and two parks. It is gated from the back, but open to visitors from the front. It's on rolling hills, which most of our city is. I never understood why people would want to live on a golf course, but believe it or not, we get quite a few that do.

I hear my phone ding:

Rose: I checked with Chris. He said he'll take the day off work Tuesday, and we can go. He's more excited about this now than I am. It's crazy how that worked out.

Me: Okay, see you then!

I text Jeremy:

Me: I'm not going to be home until late. I'm showing some houses this evening, over at Marble Springs.

I'm not sure why I even said Marble Springs. It's not like he knows what I'm talking about.

Jeremy: Okay, all is fine here. I'll let the dogs out.

I look at the oversized wall clock. I realize Mr. and Mrs. Hughes will be here at any given minute. I go to the front of the building and greet them at the door. "Hi! I'm Cassie Jennings." We meet and greet, doing our salutations.

I ask, "Would you like to go in my car, or do you want to take both?"

Mr. Hughes suggests we take both cars, that way he and Mrs. Hughes can have private discussions about the houses on the way. He asks, "How many houses will we be seeing."

I answer, "Three."

Chapter 33

Albert looks at his children. "What do you want to do today?"

They're eating their breakfast and thinking it over. "Six Flags is pretty hard to beat, Dad." Randy says, as he takes another bite of his eggs.

Maggie suggests, "We could always go to the water park."

I ask, "Did you bring your swimsuits?"

"No, but we can go by the house and pick them up."

I say, "Let's see what else we can think of doing."

Joey asks, "How about we play a game?"

Maggie adds in, "Or we could go to the library and pick a book."

Randy says, "I got it. Why don't we go to Barnes & Noble? We can buy a game and play it at the coffee shop?"

I respond, "Fabulous idea! That's what we'll do. We can eat lunch at the coffee shop too. We'll save swimming for next weekend."

"Ewww coffee," Joey replies.

"They serve more than coffee silly. They have juices and waters there too. They also have cake, cookies, and other stuff." Maggie's eyebrows go up and down in excitement, as she tells Joey about all the goodies.

All the kids will have something to do, and if Randy gets bored, there's a Best Buy next door. I'm sure Maggie will be busy drinking her juice and reading her book. They also have toys, so I know Joey will be distracted trying to choose one. After they wear themselves out a bit, we can play a game.

When we arrive, all the kids go their separate ways. I tell Joey, "It's okay if you wander off by yourself, but don't go by the front doors. When you're finished, you come look for me. I'll be at the coffee shop." I point in its direction.

His eyes are preoccupied when he says, "Okay, Daddy."

I go up and order a plain black coffee. I look at the pastries and decide to wait for dessert. I want to eat it with the kids. I walk over to the new release books, which is right by the coffee shop, so I don't worry about Joey not seeing me. I go through an assortment and choose, "The Valet." It's a crime mystery and looks interesting. I love the way it starts with a woman in stilettos, killing men.

I sit back down at a big, round table. I sip my coffee and do some reading. Maggie joins me. I pass her a five, and she orders herself a juice. She comes back and sits with me. "What book did you pick out, Maggie?"

"I picked out, "Crooked Hills," by Cullen Bunn. It's an adventure book, Dad. I've already read four pages of it while I was standing. Imagine how much I'll read now that I'm sitting... and with a juice. I feel like I'm in the best dream ever!"

I smile at her, thinking of how dramatic girls can be. I take another drink of my coffee and finish reading my chapter before Joey walks over to us. He takes a seat and huffs and puffs because he's stuck between two toys to buy. "Look Daddy, and I found a comic book!"

Joey holds it up, all proud, "Democritus Brand and the Endless Machine." He then reads the authors, "It's by Cullen Bunn and JimmyZ Johnston."

"That's coincidental. Your sister has a book by Cullen Bunn as well. He must be popular." I look around for Randy. I don't see him. "Do you want something to drink, Joey?"

"Nah, I'm not thirsty just yet. I'll wait for Randy, then I'll get something." No sooner does he say that, and Randy comes walking up to us.

He pulls a chair out and smiles. I love when Randy smiles. At his age, he's not an easy teen to please. "I didn't find a book that caught my interest," he says excitedly and continues, "but I found a record by the Beetles!"

I'm rather surprised he picked the Beetles. They've been around from generation to generation. I ask Randy, "Are you still spinning on that old record player I got you about five years ago?"

"Yep, but I got it some Bose Speakers and it sounds like new. You wouldn't believe the bass that comes out of it." He gets quiet for a moment and then says, "I just need to update my record collection. I had no idea they sold them here."

I ask, "What do you say we all have some dessert and clean up and play a game?"

They're all full of nods. "Did any of you look at the games?"

They're shaking their heads no, and Maggie says, "I was waiting for you guys."

About thirty minutes after desserts, we're standing in front of the games. We need one that's not too verbal, so we don't get anyone at the coffee shop upset, yet one that is fun and interactive. We decide on Ticket to Ride, First Journey. It's a game that you collect cards of different colors and use them to claim railway routes with your trains. You complete your tickets to achieve victory.

I hold it up for the three kids to see, "How's this?"

Chapter 34

The Hughes didn't like any of the three houses I showed them. I have the list of houses ready for Chris and Rose, though. I'm amped up on showing these cabins to them. It's right in their price range, and they have gorgeous views. One is across the lake from us. I think I'll show them it last. To me, it's the best one.

I pick up my phone, but before calling them I ask Jeremy, "Do you want to go with me to show Chris and Rose the cabins?"

He says, "Sure, I'm curious."

He still doesn't have his memory back, but he's getting more and more comfortable being with me. I tell him, "I was hoping you'd say that because I think you'll really enjoy yourself." I look at him, "One of the reasons I became a real estate agent was opening the doors to new surprises."

An hour and a phone call later and we're on the road to meet Chris and Rose. I'm so excited. I'm singing and dancing as I'm driving. Jeremy just laughs at me. "What, you're not going to join in on my own personal concert starring moi?"

He responds, "I wouldn't want to ruin it for you."

We get to the top of hill, and I see Rose. "Where's Chris, I thought you said he was coming?"

"He's more excited than me, he wouldn't miss this for the world. He just took a little hike through the tree line. He said he'll be back in a minute."

I show them the mailboxes. "Up here is where you'll collect your mail. Oh, and there's a big dumpster on the other side of the property, but I'll show you that when I give you a tour."

Rose says, "I can't wait!!!" She calls into the woods, "Hurry up, Chris."

Right about then, Chris comes walking out, "Hold your horses already. I said I'd be back in a few minutes. Geez." He looks in my direction, "Cassie, the woods are spectacular here. I even noticed a deer stand. Are we allowed to hunt?"

I explain to him, "Not inside the electric gated area, but there's land surrounding it. I could find out who owns it and see if they'd let you."

"Well, hunting isn't my main objective. Having a nice place for Rose and myself is."

"Do you want to leave your car here and we can all get in mine?"

Rose and Chris look at each other and say, "Sure."

I show them three of the cabins before we get to the last one. I think they're going to love it! They're excited about the three I've shown them, but I know this one will take their breath away. I tell them, "I saved the best for last. At least, in my opinion."

Chris says, "I don't know how it can get any better than the last one." He adds, "I'm basically sold on it. It's also twenty grand less than what we planned to spend, which means we can work on it if we want. Maybe we can add a garage."

"We will see about that. This one is across the lake from where Jeremy and I are building our house. We'll be looking at the same lake, just from different directions."

Rose laughs and says, "We can boat to each other."

I laugh and tell Rose, "Hell, the dam is what the walking to each other would be for."

I wind the car around the view of the dam I'm talking to her about. We get to a large cottage that has a garden shed. I already see Rose checking it out. I go through the keys, until I get to the right ones. I grab the folder with all my paperwork just in case they have any questions I don't know the answer to. As I unlock the door, it reveals a large, beautiful living room. There's a hand carved tree trunk near the staircase. It goes all the way up to the second floor. Rose says, "Wow."

I tell them, "The owner of this one is a wood carver. He did all the work to this place on his own." I can tell Chris and Rose are enthralled.

When Rose enters the kitchen, she calls out, "Oh my gosh, Chris!!! Come look at this kitchen."

The cabinets are all custom made. There are tiny carvings of a lion around each knob. The floor's wood matches the cabinet, and the countertops are all made of brown and white granite. The majority being white with brownish-beige streaks going through it. The kitchen sink is a double. It has a pull-down sprayer. There's a huge arched breakfast counter that wraps itself around the entire kitchen cooking area. It has plenty of cabinetry to store goodies in. It also has a washroom off the kitchen, with a desk area for recipes. The appliances are all updated and matching stainless steel. The double oven is made into the wall. I mean, if we weren't building a house, I'd want to buy this one.

Chris asks, "How much?"

I tell him it's right at his budget price of two hundred and twenty thousand. I then say, "I think we could get him down twenty grand."

"Yeah, this place is not notorious for garages, and I'd like to build one. I noticed a place on the left, where there's plenty of room for one."

"Well, they probably didn't have garages because this used to be a camping ground. These were cabins people rented out, until Annie Mae bought it out and turned it into a quaint subdivision in the woods. Most of the cabins have been renovated to live in, but they weren't always this nice. She and her husband, Will, have done a lot of work."

Rose comes from upstairs and says, "Can we put a bid on it, honey?"

Chris looks at me, and I nod. I put the paperwork on the countertop, and we fill out the necessary paperwork. Chris says, "Thanks for doing this for us."

I smile at him and Rose, and say, "You're welcome. I'm just glad to have friendly neighbors nearby."

Jeremy finally speaks up, and says, "Congratulations on finding one you like. It's gorgeous!"

"Yeah man, I can definitely see us having game nights. I can see Rose having a wonderful time, and cooking with me in the kitchen. I can see a future here. I just hope they take our offer."

I let him know, "Sales have been down this time of year. It's spring, so the rain kind of makes it slow. I think they'll take it or come back with something that'll perk your interest."

Rose asks, "Have you heard anything more about Alicia?"

As I lock the door, I answer, "No. I'm going to call her mom this evening and see if she has any more information."

Chris asks, "Do you guys want to grab a bite to eat?"

Chapter 35

It's been a crazy, long morning. Tomorrow is Jeremy's doctor appointment. I'm glad, I'd like to find out why his memory hasn't come back yet. It's been longer than Dr. Remeke projected. I want my house finished, I want the wedding, and I even want a baby. It all seems lost now. Where's my Jeremy?!

Today, I'm going to show the Hughes some houses again. They want to be in the county, so there's not a lot to choose from there. There is a residential area in it, overlooking a community lake. I think they might like that. It's country living, but right in the city! It's a little more than their budget, but for the price, you get a lot of house. That's exactly what Mrs. Hughes wanted! Let's hope this one works out because they wouldn't be too happy with the other choices. I call them up, and we schedule a showing at 1 pm. That's right after lunch.

I ring up Rose, "Hey, it's me. Do you want to grab lunch? The owners made a counteroffer, and I thought we could talk about it in person."

"Sure, but Chris isn't home. I can't make any decisions without him. It just wouldn't be fair. We can discuss it though, and I can always call him to see what he says."

"See you at 11:30?"

"11:30 it is." I hear the phone click, and I hurry to get dressed. I've been lounging in my gray sweats and green sweater all day, looking like a total bum. It was pure comfort while it lasted. I put on some presentable dress-wear because I'll meet the Hughes right after Rose.

"Jeremy, I'm going out. The owners of the River Hill cabin made an offer. I pause a moment, waiting to see if he wants to say anything, which he doesn't. "I think they should take it."

"Have fun. Will Chris be there?"

"No, he's at work, but Rose said she can call him with the counteroffer. I guess we'll see. Oh, and afterward, I'm meeting the Hughes. I have a great house to show them, and we can certainly use the money. We're into our savings now."

"I feel like a lazy bum, who sits on his ass all day. I definitely need to get back to work, but I don't know what I'm doing."

I'm suddenly full of compassion, and I explain to him, "You have a doctor's appointment tomorrow. Maybe Dr. Remeke can tell us more about your condition, or at least explain why it's taken longer than he thought. I know this is hard on you too. Especially sitting at home and having nothing to do."

"Yeah, I think I'll take the dogs for a long walk today."

I grab my purse, my two folders with the house addresses labeled on it, and my keys. I feel bad for Jeremy to be stuck at home all day, but I'm not sure what to do about it. I guess I could have taken him to work with me, but I think he would have been bored. Also, I'm not sure how the Hughes would have felt about it.

I pull up to the Coffee Brewery. As I'm getting out, I see the guy that Jeremy hit. What was his name?! Oh yeah, Albert, Albert Wilson! As he's walking by, he stops in place, "Is that you, Cassie?" I still don't remember telling him my name, which really creeps me out.

"Hi, Albert. How are you doing?" I notice he also has a bandage on his head.

"Other than a few broken ribs and a headache, I'm great." He looks me over from my head to my toes. Again, I'm left uncomfortable.

"Well, heh, I better get inside. I'm meeting with a friend."

"Before you go... How's Jeremy doing?"

I bite my lip for a second, then I say, "He still doesn't have his memory back. He's getting restless, but he's okay."

"Okay, I better get off to work. I don't want to be late."

I continue inside, and I see Rose at our usual corner table by the window. "Hey lady! Got some good news for you."

She says, "First, coffee. I've been craving one of theirs all day."

Once we get our pastries and coffees, we take a seat. "Before we eat, let me tell you the counteroffer."

She says, "Okay," as she pushes her cinnamon roll away.

I smile and say, "Two hundred and ten thousand." I take a sip of my coffee and show her the paperwork. "What do you think?"

She picks up her phone excitedly, "I think I can't wait to tell Chris!"

As she's talking to Chris she says, "Hold on one second, hun." She looks at me, "Chris said he can meet us here for lunch and sign the papers with me."

"Wonderful!"

As we wait, I tell Rose, "They still haven't found Alicia."

Rose finishes chewing and then says, "I know it's unbelievable. I miss her so much."

I conclude, "Me too."

We make small talk until Chris arrives. By the time he does, we're done eating. "Sorry we didn't wait for you, but we didn't know you were coming. The pastries would have been stale."

"That's fine. I wasn't planning on staying that long. I just came by to sign the papers." Chris smiles at Rose, and then at me. "I can't wait!" All the stuff is moved out of the place, so it's move-in ready for them. I feel a tinge of jealousy, wishing I could get in my house that was built for us.

"Okay, sign right here... and here... oh, and here." They both take turns sprawling their signatures across the pages.

I go home. I'm hoping Jeremy got his memory back, but since there was no phone call, it's highly unlikely. The dogs come running toward me like I'm the best thing that ever happened to them. "It's good seeing you boys too. I've missed you." I pet each one on the head and grab Columbo's tail. "Got you!" He playfully wags it, as I let it go.

I call out, "Jeremy?"

He says, "I'm in here." He's in our bedroom, changing out of sweatpants. "I went for a hike with the boys, and they decided to get too close to the lake. They got mud all over their paws, then wiped them clean on my clothes. But!!! I did get good slobber kisses." We both laugh. "I used the shower earlier."

He doesn't have a shirt on, and I can't help but stare. "Do you want me to get the couch ready for you?"

"I thought if you didn't mind, I could try sleeping on the bed with you tonight?" We look at each other awkwardly.

"Sure, if you're comfortable with that." I think to myself, am I comfortable with that? I've been sleeping alone for a while now. I've kind of adjusted to it.

I go into the bathroom to put my pajamas on. I'm sure he doesn't feel comfortable sleeping how we normally do, naked. I take my make up off and look at myself in the mirror. Not only am I aging, but it's like I'm aging without Jeremy. I know it hasn't been that long, but it feels like forever. I've never been without him for any span of time.

When I snuggle into the covers, Jeremy is all the way on his side of the bed. He's stiff as a board. I'm used to Jeremy pulling me into his arms and holding me. It's just weird. I turn the lamp off that's on the nightstand. He turns his off.

"Oh, guess who I bumped into at the Coffee Brewery today?"

He asks, "Who?"

"Albert Wilson, the guy that had the collision with you. He said other than a few broken ribs and a head bump, he's alright. He asked how you were doing."

Chapter 36

By the time I get the kids back to their mother, it's late. I'm feeling a surge of energy. I decide to go by Cassie's place. Maybe I can get a peek at her through the windows. She will give me something to dream about tonight.

When I get there, I don't see anyone. I just see that the bedroom light is on. I stay for about an hour, until I see the light go off. I guess she's going to bed earlier than usual. I decide to drive back home.

As I arrive, I remember her panties that I have tucked inside my pillowcase. Next, I'd like to get a shirt to lie down next to, or better yet one of her nighties. I can feel myself get excited at just the thought of Cassie. I want her so bad.

The apartment is dark until I turn the living room light on. I go over to the windows and close the blinds. I go inside the kids' rooms and make their beds. I tidy them up, then find myself on the couch relaxing.

I go through a few channels before seeing Alicia's photograph on the tv. The news is asking everyone for information related to her, to step forward. Little do they know, nobody saw me. I'm safe. I flip through a few more channels until I reach a movie.

An hour goes by before the movie finishes. I get in bed, take her panties out of the pillowcase, and smell them. I must have fallen asleep because I open my eyes, and the sun is beaming down on me.

I get up, enter the living room, and open my blinds. I make some coffee and wait for it to finish brewing. Once it does, I take it to the table in front of the windows, and I sit, watching people come and go from the shops. I wonder where some are headed off to, while listening to the mumbles of chatting, as they sit outside on the round tables in front of the side stage. This is a very nice place to live. During the summer weekends, they put on concerts for adults and kids. I haven't seen one yet, but there's one happening this weekend. I won't have the kids until the following weekend.

The home phone rings. "Hello?"

"This is Doctor Govatz's office. The doctor would like you to come in. She wants to talk to you about some tests."

I explain, "I'm off work today. Is it possible to schedule me in?"

She says, "Let me see if I can do some rearranging. I'm not sure if I can, but I will try. Then, I will call you back."

I answer, "Thank you."

I hang up the phone and feel my heart sinking. Whenever a doctor wants to talk to you in person it's usually bad news. Especially when it's about tests that have been done.

I need to stick around the house, but my nervous energy wants to be anywhere else. I look at the phone, feeling vulnerable. I hope she can see me today. I can't see myself surviving in the not know for very long. If she can't, maybe I can sign a paper for information over the telephone.

That's when my phone rings again. "Hello?"

"This is Dr. Govatz's office. I'm calling you back to inform you she can see you today. How about four o'clock?"

"Yes, sure. Four o'clock is great. Thank you."

"Dr. Govatz will see you at four o'clock this afternoon."

I hang up the phone, feeling petrified. I decide to grab my hat and go downstairs for the next cup of coffee. That's when I bump into Cassie. I'm a little surprised because she's finally without that man, Jeremy. We are standing so close I could kiss her. Our shoulders are touching. After we talk, she leaves. I go inside and get myself a coffee and sit at the umbrella table outside. It's such a nice day. Cassie made me forget all about my doctor appointment for a few minutes. She has that effect on me.

By the time four o'clock rolls around, I'm at the doctor's office in the waiting room. I'm next to be seen. It was crowded, but I didn't expect less. I did make the appointment at the last minute for the same day.

A nurse walks out, "Albert Wilson."

"That's me." I stand up and follow her through the door into a long, narrow hall. She stops at a scale. She instructs me to stand on it, and I end up weighing 180 lbs. Not bad for being fifty-two. The wait in the little room was agonizing. I have a feeling hereafter will be much the same.

I can hear the chart coming off my door and the doctor going through papers, as they fumble against each other. "Albert Wilson?" She asks.

I'm sitting on the chair against the wall, "Yes, that's me."

She sits on a stool and rolls it over in front of me. "I'm sure you remember me. I'm Dr. Govatz."

I rub my chin and answer, "Yes."

"I have some bad news. We found a brain tumor. We'd like to run some more tests to see if it's malignant."

All I basically heard was brain tumor. There's no use asking if it's cancerous because she doesn't know yet. "How am I supposed to sleep tonight?" I know all I'll be thinking about is the tumor. Oh, there's a concert tonight! Maybe that'll take my mind off it.

She swivels to her computer, "I can prescribe you some sleeping pills. How about Ambien? Have you taken it before?"

"No, I've never needed sleeping pills before. I may not need them now. I'm just worried I'll be up all night, tossing and turning, thinking about the damn tumor."

"Well, Ambien you can take as needed. If you sleep, don't take it. If you can't, you'll have it."

"When do you want me to come in for the tests?"

She swivels her stool back toward me, "We don't do the tests here. I'll make you an appointment at the proper clinics. They'll call you to confirm them. If the dates and times don't work out, just rearrange them."

As I'm leaving, I feel at a loss. I don't physically feel any different, so I doubt it's malignant. It's still depressing just knowing I have a tumor growing on my brain. How strange! I debate telling the wife and decide I'm in no mood to deal with her. I fill the prescription at the pharmacy. I go home and get ready for the concert. It's supposed to be a bluesy band.

An hour later, and I'm early for the concert. I wanted to get a table. I sip on my coffee, waiting for the entertainment to start. Most of the shops are closed, but not Bar Louie's. It'll probably be open until one o'clock in the morning. I never stay up that late, so I'm not sure. Right as I'm debating the time, the music starts.

I hear people laughing and talking. I can see people dancing and walking. Some are standing behind the stage, but most are standing in front of it. I let out a big sigh, as if my one breath carries all its problems within it. My shoulders start to loosen up. I close my eyes and take in the saxophone.

Chapter 37

Sleeping next to Jeremy was so weird! It was like sleeping next to a stranger. I didn't even wake up snuggled to him. I felt like I was cheating on him. I was all the way to the left, and he was all the way to the right. I'm glad his doctor appointment is today.

I quietly get up to go to the bathroom. I find an outfit and decide to put on some coffee and make breakfast. As I'm frying the bacon, he comes in from behind me and kisses the top of my head. I thought I had my Jeremy back for a second, but I turned around and he was somewhat blushing. He asks, "How are you coping with me being like this?"

As I turn the bacon, I tell him, "I'm not going to lie, it's tough. I miss my Jeremy. Last night it felt like I was cheating on him... you. Weird right?!"

He pours himself a cup of coffee, "Not weird at all. I'm at a loss myself. I keep trying to think of work, things I used to do, and I keep hoping something dawns on me."

"I keep forgetting and losing things lately too. This morning I went to put on my favorite," I stop myself feeling embarrassed, "undergarment, and I'm missing it. It matches my bra. I know it was in the drawer, or so I thought it was. I even checked the hamper."

He looks up at me and smiles, "Things happen. Maybe your panties are lost in the sock drawer."

I pour myself a mug of coffee too. "Maybe. Oh, don't forget your doctor's appointment is today."

"I didn't. I dressed comfortable for it. It's strange going

through his closet. He has a lot of nice clothes and barely any sweats. I feel like I love sweats, especially these ones." He brushes over his leg with his hand. "His! I mean mine."

"I keep doing that too. Him, you... I get what you mean. Your appointment isn't until 1 pm." I make him a plate and put it on the table. "We have plenty of time to eat."

I join him, and I scrape around my eggs a little. "Can't remember nothing at all, huh?"

He shakes his head no. "Not even the smallest details. It's black when I think back. I know it sounds strange, but it almost makes me feel dizzy."

After breakfast, we play with the dogs outside. Something Jeremy rarely did. He was always on the go or spending the much-needed time with me.

I look at my watch, "I guess we better clean up a bit and get ready to go." By the time we're done playing fetch and tag, it's already noon.

When we arrive at the doctor's clinic, there's not that many people in front of us. Maybe because they just had lunch, but for whatever reason, I'm relieved. I thought we'd have to sit there thirty minutes before they could even take us to the back.

When they call his name, we both stand, but he holds his hand out. "I'd like to do this alone." My feelings are hurt, but I mean it is his choice. I had a few questions myself, but I'm not going to argue about it.

While he goes in the back, I look through the magazine rack. I should have brought a book, but I didn't want to leave poor Jeremy just sitting there... like he just did to me. I go through my phone applications to see what's going on with our families on iBook. Photos of traveling abroad. Photos of Rv'ing. Both of our parents look happy.

Jeremy's mom is hoping that when she returns from Bermuda that he will have his memory back. She's not hoping nearly as much as I am. Sometimes it feels like Jeremy has a twin brother. I sit back down with my magazine and find myself flipping through the pages, wondering why Jeremy didn't want me to go back there with him. Does he find me a nuisance?

An hour and a half pass before Jeremy walks back out. Dr. Remeke is by his side. I have a hundred and one questions, but I bite my tongue, keeping them to myself. Maybe Jeremy can answer them for me.

As we are walking to the car, Jeremy asks, "Do you want to get something to eat? I'm starving."

I suggest, "We could go to Zeniros for lunch. They're a bit expensive, but oh so good!"

"We haven't splurged since I lost my memory. Let's do it."

My phone rings, "Hello?"

"Cassie. This is the Donahues. We're calling to see if you found any listings we can look at. We found a couple online ourselves. We were wondering if you could get the keys too, so we can see them in person?"

"Hi, Mrs. Donahue! You'll be happy to know I found two within the area you're looking for. Sure, I could get the keys if you could text me the listing numbers or the addresses. I'd jot them down now, but I'm driving."

She didn't sound very happy. I was glad to get off the phone with her. I mean, she's always been uptight, but this time she made it sound like I wasn't doing my job. Yet, they were the ones who didn't have time to look at the listings today. They set it for tomorrow.

I'm anxious to ask Jeremy what the doctor said. I decide to wait until we are sitting inside the restaurant. Please, oh please, don't say you're in a permanent state of mind. I'm not even sure if the two of us can start from scratch and fall back in love. At least, I don't think I could with this new Jeremy. He's not the same.

We get to Zeniros, and two gals, one of which is in training, lead us to a table. We make our drink orders, and as soon as they're gone, I ask, "Well!!! What did Dr. Remeke say?"

He takes my hand into his, "He said to give it more time and stop trying to rush it. He seems confident I'll get my memory back. Also, the rest of the tests came back without any abnormalities. I'm okay." He smiles. "I'm so relieved. With this memory loss, I thought maybe internal bleeding."

I look down at his hand that's holding mine and back up to meet his eyes, "That's great news Jeremy. Does he have any time range of when you might get your memory back?"

He lets go of my hand and takes a drink of water, "Actually, after he lectured me, I didn't ask."

How could he not ask! Doesn't he know I'm going insane without my Jeremy! Can I afford to financially support us if we run out of our savings? If we use all our savings, will we have enough money to get married? I feel savage for not caring more about how he must be feeling right now, but this is our future together. Nothing makes sense. I feel at a loss.

Chapter 38

Last night, I pretended to fall asleep on the couch, just so I wouldn't have to sleep on the bed with him again. It was too awkward. I love Jeremy, but it's like being with his brother or something. It's just too weird for me to accept. I guess I'm going to have to have a talk with him about it. Maybe I'll do that over breakfast.

I look at the clock on the tv and realize I'm going to be late for the Donahues if I don't get up and get dressed! I tug the covers off me and run my fingers through my messy hair, from tossing and turning on the couch last night.

I knock on the bathroom door, but to my surprise Jeremy isn't in there. Where is he? I call for the dogs, but they're not inside either. I figure Jeremy must have taken them for a walk. I go into the kitchen and look out the back window. They're not in the yard. I look for the leashes. They're gone! Just as I figured, a walk.

I take a quick shower and put on a matching suit skirt, with a white silk blouse. By the time I'm done with my hair, Jeremy is back with the dogs. I grab my folder and keys, "I have to go. I'm almost running late."

He just laughs and says, "Okay."

I add, "I'll stop by the grocery store on my way home."

On my way to the first listing, I keep peeking over to the passenger seat and fumbling through papers in my folder. I'm trying to find the right listing for the address. We are going to see the two I found first. Then, we will see the two they found online. I'm curious to see what caught their interests. I should have sorted through these damn papers before I left.

I get to the listing, and it's even prettier in person than it is in the picture. It's a Colonial home. It's right at their price range too. My phone rings:

"Hello?"

"Cassie, it's Rose. We are moving next Friday!!!! I'm so excited. Can you help us?"

"Sure, I can't stay on the phone, though. I'm meeting with clients right now."

"Oops, sorry! Talk to you later."

I put my phone in my suit jacket pocket and pull the papers for this house. Here it is. 4 bedrooms and three baths. It has 3200 square feet. There's a finished basement. It has a fenced-in yard, surrounded by conservation land. I think they'll like this one. Though, I didn't save the best for last. I see the Donahues pull up. I instantly notice her pointing toward the front porch, showing it to her husband.

"Mr. and Mrs. Donahue. It's nice seeing you again." We shake hands, meeting and greeting each other. "I think you'll find what you want in this house. Also, it's right at your price range. It's turnkey, so there's no work that needs to be done."

After I unlock it, I leave it to them to wander around with each other, taking in what they do and do not like. After about thirty minutes, Mr. Donahue comes into the kitchen where I'm sitting and waiting patiently. He says, "You've done great, Cassie. This isn't what we want, though. My wife was hoping for a bigger porch."

"Okay, let me lead you to the second listing."

They follow me to about six blocks away. I get out and wait for them. "This is an old-style English home." I open the paperwork for this listing. "It has five bedrooms and four and half baths. It has a big backyard. Unfortunately, it's not fenced in because they grow thorn bushes around the property. It is, however, twenty thousand dollars below your price range. You could always tear down the thorn bush and put up a fence!"

Mrs. Donahue says, "This is gorgeous! If the inside is as nice as the outside, I'm going to fall in love with it."

Mr. Donahue takes his wife by the waist. "Now, now Nancy, don't get your hopes up."

She says, "Hopes? Look at this place! It's gorgeous," she says, as she takes a rose from the garden and holds it gently in the palm of her hand.

I turn the key and we all go inside. It takes my breath away. We enter an open foyer that has an old walnut door. It leads to a coat closet. Then, as we step through, we enter the living room. It has a wood burning fireplace, and there's a small, spacious offset office room adjoined to it. To the left, there's a kitchen. The only separation is the kitchen island. It's nice because you can see the fireplace from the kitchen. The living room windows are smaller than most homes being built now, but they have stained glass windows.

I take a seat at the island. There's no furniture left, but there are two breakfast counter stools. I was glad to see they left on the utilities. It's always easier showing the homes when I can flick on the lights. It also helps when it's warm.

Mrs. Donahue comes downstairs, jabbering away to her husband about how she loves this English style home. They go into the backyard, and I look over the paperwork for the two homes they picked out to see. I notice they're waterfront homes, which they didn't mention wanting to be located by water. Also, one is in the valley of the subdivision called Garrett. The other is in the same subdivision, but it's located on a hill.

We go to the house in the valley first. I note that it only has three bedrooms and two baths, which surprises me that they'd look at it. The windows overlooking the lake are beautiful. The kitchen is tiny, though. I can already tell this house is not going to do it for them. They don't stay upstairs very long. Mrs. Donahue says, "Let's see the other one."

We drive up a huge hill. The views from the top are absolutely beautiful. You can see rolling hills upon hills of newer built homes. I open the lock box, and we enter. We first walk into the kitchen. It's not an open floor plan, but each window I can see has a beautiful view of the sky... unless you get closer. Then, you can see down to the tops of other homes. This house is furnished. I guess it's still occupied by the owners. I take a seat on the recliner. As I wait, I check my phone.

I text Rose:

Me: I'll call you as soon as I'm done. I'm showing the last listing now.

The Donahues come inside from the deck. Mr. Donahue says, "I love this view." Mrs. Donahue and I both nod our heads in agreement. "However, Mrs. Donahue is sold on the Old English Colonial."

Mrs. Donahue's smile stretches across her face, "I sure am!"

Mr. Donahue says, "We'd like to put a bid on it."

"Do you want to come back to my office, or do it here?"

He replies, "Here is fine."

"Okay, let me go to my car and grab the needed paperwork for a bid."

I come back inside, we fill out the paperwork, and then we scratch a few John Henrys... and it's ready to turn in. We say our goodbyes, and off I am on my way back home. It's been a long day.

I call Rose, "Hey girl! Just put the Donahues bid in. That's another house!"

She sounds excited, "I can't wait! We did it. We're moving into our own place, Cassie! Can you believe it?!"

"You deserve it, Rose. You've been waiting and saving for quite a few years."

"Yeah, but this home is so much more than I ever thought we could afford."

I make my way inside. "I'm home and there's no sign of

Jeremy. I better get off here and see if I can find him."
    "Okay girl, talk to you later."

Chapter 39

The concert was great. It was just what I needed to take my mind off things. Women dancing everywhere and children laughing. If only Cassie would have been there with me! I need to go to the office and pick up some paperwork. Let's see, it's Monday. Afterward, I'll swing by her place and see if she's home.

The office is quiet. It's only two blocks from where I'm living now. It's convenient for me. Everything is really, besides Cassie. If this guy weren't in the way, she'd be easier. As I walk outside and try to get into my car, a vehicle swerves, almost hitting me. I realize I have to take my mind off Cassie for now. She's like tequila rose... seductive, delicious, and dangerous.

I park my car down the way, so I'm not obvious. I guess I didn't park far enough down because that guy, Jeremy, comes out of the house. He walks straight toward me. I'm nervous as hell. I'm not sure what I'm going to say. He says, "What are you doing parked here?"

I wipe a few sweat tears from my brow, hoping he doesn't notice and explain, "I heard this place might be coming up for sale soon, and I wanted to take a look at it."

"Oh," he gets quiet and looks back toward the estate. "Well, would you like to come in for a tour? I'm not doing anything."

"I wouldn't want to bother you."

"It's no bother. I won't take no for an answer. Let me just put my dogs outside, and I'll meet you at the front door."

Jeremy makes his way back.

I get in my vehicle and pull into the driveway. I quickly debate getting rid of him now, while the opportunity has presented itself to me. I walk up to his front porch, and he opens the door for me. "Cassie, my fiancé, isn't home right now. You'll have to excuse the paw prints on the floor. We have three dogs that think they're human."

"I'm basically curious of the lay out." He shows me room to room. When we get upstairs to the bedroom, I feel excited. I could bash him over his stupid head now, but what if someone saw my car parked outside in the driveway.

His phone rings. "I'll be right back." He leaves me alone in the bedroom. I quickly go to the dresser and fumble through the drawers. Aha! I find one of her silk nighties. I tuck it into my pants. It's small, thin, and no big deal to hide. He's still talking on his cell phone when he walks back in.

I go to the master bath. So, this is where my girl takes her showers. I see there are two wardrobe rooms and double sinks. I'm pleasantly surprised the window blinds are open. I look out and see there are woods facing it. I'll have to keep that in mind. I walk back out of the bath.

Jeremy puts his phone in his pocket, "Sorry, that was my doctor making another appointment for some more tests he wants done."

"That's quite alright. I know all about doctors and tests."

He asks, "You do?"

"Yeah, apparently I have a tumor." It feels weird telling someone that. He's the first, and out of all the people to tell, I'm surprised at myself.

Jeremy looks lost in thought for a moment and then says, "Would you like a cup of coffee? My fiancé isn't due back for a couple more hours, and the truth is, it gets quiet around here."

I follow him into the kitchen, "Sure."

"You look familiar to me. Which is a nice change! Maybe

I've seen you around the doctors' offices?" He pours me a cup and hands it to me. He asks, "Crème or sugar?"

"No thanks. I like mine black as onyx." I play dumb. "Why are you in and out of the doctor's for?"

"I have amnesia. It should be gone by now, but I still have no recollection of anything from my past." He takes another drink of coffee. "All the tests so far have come back good, so the doctor is unsure why I haven't regained my memory."

I speak up, "This tumor of mine, we're not sure if it's malignant yet. I should be getting a call anytime now with an update. I don't feel any different. It seems like if it were cancerous, I'd be experiencing some side effects from it. Dizziness, etc. etc."

"So, to change the subject to something more pleasant than our trauma... What did you think of the house?"

I slide the empty coffee cup back to him, "It's quaint. I really like it and will have to tell the kids about it. Right now, we're in a wonderful apartment. I'm in no hurry to leave it."

He says, "Well, that's a good thing. With no recollection, it's hard for me to make decisions now, based on what I would have. If that makes any sense!"

I respond, "Yeah, I know what you mean." I stand up, "I best be going. I still have some errands to run. Thanks for showing me the place." He shows me out and waves good-bye.

Chapter 40

With Jeremy's condition, I always feel disappointment when I walk back in the house, and he still has no memory. It's as if it's dragging on. I want to shake him and say, give me back my Jeremy. Where are you?

I call his name through the house, but he doesn't respond. I check outside, and he's not out there with the dogs. I let them in. I wonder how long they've been in the backyard. I go into the bedroom and see his shoes are missing. He's went somewhere. I try calling his cell phone, but it goes to messages. That's not what I want.

I start to feel a little frantic, but then he walks through the door, "Oh hey, Cassie. You're home a little early?"

I feel a sigh of relief come over me. "I was worried about you. I couldn't find you."

He says, "I went for a hike. I would have brought the three dogs, but I didn't really feel like untangling their leashes."

"Do you want to go to River Hill property with me? I need to take some measurements and order us a refrigerator for the house. We're definitely going with stainless steel."

"I know this is going to sound strange, but won't Jeremy be mad if you're making decisions without him?"

A half smile curls on my lips, "No, he won't be upset about the appliances. He would have had me pick them anyway." I twirl my hair up in a bun. "It seems strange, staring right at you and talking about him in second person."

"I know. This whole thing is strange. I'm not sure where

it is I fit in. Like, am I going to remember this talk? Or will I just go back to before the car crash?"

"So, are ya coming with? Or staying behind?"

"Definitely, coming with!" He walks into the bedroom. "Just give me a few minutes to change my clothes."

I check the refrigerator. I need to stop by the grocery store and the winery. "Our parents have sure been quiet. They normally call to check on us by now. Not that I don't appreciate the phone not ringing a dozen times."

He calls back out, "I hardly ever hear the phone ring." Then he says, "Oh, that reminds me! A man came by for a tour. He said he heard our house was going to be for sale and wanted to see it."

I walk into the bedroom with a puzzled expression, "What? What man? I haven't told anyone. Well, except Rose and Chris. They may have mentioned it to someone."

"Yeah, it was weird. He was just parked, and I asked him what he was doing. He said he wanted to see the place, so I offered him a tour. It wasn't like I was doing anything."

"You need to be more careful about inviting strangers inside our home, though. It's unsettling." I lecture him, as if he's a little boy.

He says, "Yeah, I guess you're right. Sorry about that. I had just assumed he was a friend of a friend."

We head out the door and get in my car. "Shit, I forgot the measuring tape." I run back inside to grab it.

He replies, "I thought I was the one with the memory problems."

When we get to the property, it's vacant. None of the workers are there. We go inside, and I take measurements of where the refrigerator will be. The cooktop is rather basic. It goes on the island. The double oven is on the wall. There's really nothing more to measure, except for the washer and dryer. Jeremy needs to help me choose because we were stuck choosing between two of them. I guess I could just go with his, and he'll be happy. I really want to get this done so it's move in ready.

After I take the measurements, I find Jeremy standing on the porch outside. He says, "Tranquil."

"I'm done. Do you feel like a trip to Sears?"

He answers, "Sure." We walk to the car, and he asks, "Do you have an idea of the kind of refrigerator you want?"

"I'm thinking double door with the freezer at the bottom. I saw some touch screen ones, but I don't want to go that fancy, in case it has electrical problems."

When we get inside the department store, I'm surprised by how many choices they have. I find a simple double door refrigerator. No smart stuff on it. "What do you think of this one?" I look over the measurements.

He answers, "Looks good to me."

"This is our first official buy together for our house since you've lost your memory."

He says, "Sure is."

I talk to the appliance section clerk. I tell her what I want and sign up for a delivery date. The soonest they can get it there is next week. We go through a few dates, and we finally agree on one. I can tell Jeremy is getting impatient, so I'm glad when she hands me a receipt and proof of date.

The drive home is pretty quiet. I feel as if Jeremy is upset with me, and I'm not sure why. I finally blow out some steam and ask, "Are you mad at me?"

He responds, "No, I'm not mad at you. I'm tired of being this way. I feel like it's never going to be over." He cracks his window open, "It makes me feel a little frustrated, so excuse me if I seem annoyed."

Chapter 41

Between Jeremy's mood swings and my own emotional havoc, I'm starting to feel depressed. On the upside, the Donahues and Flanagans settled on a housing price. It looks like I sold yet another one! Marge, my boss, is proud of me. Right now, with Jeremy not working, the cash flow from real estate is really helping.

Jeremy comes running in, "I know this probably isn't a lot, but I had a flashback. I remember sitting in a café with Chris, Rose and you!!!" His voice comes out a little louder than either of us expected. I can tell by the look on his face, which causes us both to laugh.

"That's exciting news, Jeremy!" I give him a hug.

"I guess from here, it's just a slow process? It was weird and almost like a dream state." He takes my hand and kisses it. "I was just putting my shoes on to take the dogs out and BAM. Just like that."

He kissed my hand, just like Jeremy used to always do. "Maybe by tomorrow you'll even remember more. That would be wonderful! Unfortunately, I have to leave. I need to have the Donahues do some final signings on the property they bought." I grab my jacket because I noticed out the window that the wind has picked up.

My drive there was shifty. It felt like the wind was blowing me all over the road. I wonder if we're under a tornado watch or warning. I turn the radio through different stations, but none of them are on the weather or news.

I'm glad when I finally arrive at the title office. I meet the

Donahues and Flanagans inside. "Hi, how are you, Mrs. Donahue?"

She leans into her husband, then holds her hands out toward me, "I'm doing fine. I'll be glad once we're all moved. I feel like my hands are drying out from packing all the cardboard boxes we've been dealing with."

Mrs. Flanagan takes a seat across from us and says, "I know what you mean. I've done so much packing lately, I'm having nightmares of drowning in boxes." She laughs. "All the empty ones tumble down over me."

"Wow, it sounds like you two have a lot in common." I pull the necessary papers out of my folder. Both the husbands and the wives sign. This is unusual for me to witness because it's usually one or the other. This is two couples at the same time, though.

When they're finished and it's notarized, I smile at them. "Enjoy your new home. Oh, and Mrs. Flanagan, have you found your place then?"

"Actually, we found a rental until we decide on one we like. We need an agent you know."

I tilt my head and say, "I happen to know a really good one." We laugh, and I hand her my card. "You'll be my only client right now. I've closed all the other buyers. I'll be completely focused on you. Call me and set up an appointment at my office, and we can go over what you're interested in and looking for."

She says, "You bet your bottom dollar."

On the drive home, I'm feeling a lot better. I had a closing, have another potential buyer, and Jeremy is getting his memory back. I feel a slight relief come over me. I pull in the driveway and park. As I get out of my car, I notice the dogs are out of the yard. "What the hell?"

I go around to the back, calling them into the fenced area, "Come on, boys." That's when I see Jeremy lying face down in the grass. I quickly go inside to get Wi-Fi signal and let the dogs in. I call the cops and tell them to send an ambulance quickly, that my fiancé is lying on the ground unconscious!

They end up keeping me on the phone with a thousand questions, like am I in any danger, etc. I explain to them I'm not. That's when an officer pulls up with an ambulance behind him. It's all happening so fast, it's hard to believe. I'm watching two men put Jeremy on a gurney. The officer says, "So you came home to him like this? Was there any sign of a break-in?"

"I only briefly went inside to use the Wi-Fi so I could call you, but nothing looked out of place. My fiancé has been experiencing amnesia from an automobile wreck he was in." I hold my hands out, "Look, I don't have time for this. Can we finish at the hospital? I really want to follow behind the ambulance."

As I'm following the ambulance at high speed, I'm stressed to the max. I'm running red lights right along with the ambulance. When we arrive at the hospital, I pull into the emergency room parking lot. I run inside, looking around for Jeremy. I call out, "Jeremy, Jeremy?"

The lady at the front desk says, "Can I help you ma'am?"

"I'm looking for Jeremy Banks. They just brought him in by ambulance."

She says, "Let me check and see what's going on, to see if I can bring you back there. Give me a minute."

She disappears into the back, and I fold my arms against my chest, trying not to panic. I breathe in through my nose and exhale out of my mouth. I tell myself don't get sick, don't get sick. She finally comes back out and tells me to follow her. I'm practically walking on her heels until we enter Jeremy's room.

He says, "Cassie!" He reaches his arms out toward me. I sink into them. "I have my memory back! I remember everything from before the wreck, but some things after the wreck are a little foggy."

Chapter 42

I went by Cassie's place to check out the tree line in front of her bedroom window. I can't believe my luck! The next thing I know Jeremy is on the ground, the dogs are loose, and Cassie comes pulling in. Before I could do anything, the police and ambulance are there. I tuck myself away inside the woods. None of them can see me, but I can see them.

Once I see Cassie follow the ambulance and police car, I slowly make my way to the backyard. I know the dogs are inside, so I go to the bedroom window. I notice it's cracked, so I open it to its fullest capacity. Before entering, I check to see if the bedroom door is closed. To my luck, it is. I remain as quiet as I can, so the dogs don't start barking.

This time, I quietly go into the bathroom and stalk her closet. I pull out one of her hoodies. Then, I make my way to her lingerie drawer. I decide to take a pair of panties and a bra. I tuck them away, and then I smell her pillow.

I climb back out through the window. The dogs hear me and start barking. I hurry and leave it cracked open, just as it was before. I leave for the tree line. I make my way back to my vehicle and hop in. The drive home was pleasantly smooth.

As I unlock my apartment, I'm grateful for it. I let out a big sigh of not being caught in the drama and throw my keys onto the countertop. I go into my bedroom and clip her bra around the extra pillow, slipping the panties over it. Then I put the hoodie down and around the pillow. There, Cassie. Now it'll be like you're lying right next to me.

Jackie Adams

I look at my watch and decide it's time I drop in at the office. I decide the walk will do me good. As I stroll along Main Street, I pass her real estate office. It's been a while since I've bumped into Cassie or seen her. I'm starting to miss her.

I walk into the office, and Cindy is there. She's our secretary. I ask, "Where's everyone at today?"

She looks at the clock. "It's almost five o'clock, Albert."

I hold out my wrist, looking at my watch, "Wow, it's that late? I didn't even realize it."

"Now that you're here, you do have three messages." She hands me a compilation of yellow sticky notes.

"Thanks, Cindy." I look through each of them. Two are from clients, and one is from my soon to be ex. I walk over to my desk and pick up the phone. First, I call the clients. The first one didn't answer, so I left a message.

The second client picks up the phone, "Hello?"

"Yes, this is Albert Wilson from Insurance Annuities. I'm returning your phone call." After a ten-minute conversation, it's decided I will come by his place and pick up his payment.

I call the wife back, "This is Albert."

"I was calling to ask you if I could keep the kids this weekend. My mother is coming in town and wants to spend time with them before she leaves. She'll only be here a few days."

"Um, yeah, I didn't have anything specific planned. As long as they're okay with it, I'm okay with it. Can I talk to them?"

She says, "They're not home. Joey is at baseball practice, Maggie is at ballet, and I never know what Randy is doing."

"Well, don't be too hard on Randy. He's turning into a man. It's all about independence at his age. Soon, he'll be getting a job and have his own money. He'll rarely be home."

She responds, "He's rarely home now."

After the phone call, I gather some papers, then walk back home. No kids this weekend. What will I do to occupy myself? Maybe I'll figure out where Cassie is going to be. If I'm missing her this much, she must be really missing me.

I get back into the apartment, kick off my shoes, and throw myself onto the couch. I flip through the channels. I see a news report on Alicia. Her whereabouts are still unknown. They're asking for anyone with information to contact the police. Same story, same bull. I find an old John Wayne western I'm content with. I watch It until I fall asleep. When I wake up, I remember my pillow. I go into the bedroom and snuggle with it.

By the time I'm awake, I realize it's time to go and see Cassie. I stretch and get dressed. I make my way downstairs to the Coffee Brewery for a black coffee and a cinnamon roll. Low and behold, there's Cassie. "Wow, look at us continuously bumping into each other."

She says, "I practically live at the Coffee Brewery."

I smile and say, "I do." I point at the ceiling. "I live upstairs."

"I was wondering why I'm always seeing you here. Now that makes sense."

I turn around to see who came in the door, and when I look back at Cassie, I spill some coffee on her shirt. "Oh no, I'm sorry."

"It's okay. I was on my way home anyway."

I tell her, "Let me make it up to you and buy you another coffee." I can tell she's getting ready to refuse me, but then I say, "I insist."

Chapter 43

I'm at the Coffee Brewery when I run into Albert, Albert Wilson. The one that got into the vehicle accident with Jeremy. He spills coffee on me and then insists on buying me another one. Against my better judgement, I accept.

They're keeping Jeremy overnight to run tests to see why he fainted, which is what they believe he did. I stopped here on my way home for some caffeine. I'm going to get him some clean clothes and feed the dogs. I also need to let them out.

"I can't stay long. I have to get back to the hospital."

He quickly asks, "Hospital?"

I explain everything that happened to Jeremy. I notice right away, Albert's a good listener. He doesn't interrupt me a single time. After I finish indulging all the information, I take a deep breath and add, "So, that's why I'm in a hurry to get back." As bad as it sounds, I'm almost glad he fainted, just because he's back to his old self.

Albert says, "Wow, talk about a lot happening in a day." He grabs my hand, "Sounds like you have your hands full."

I slide it back from under his and rest it on my lap. "Well, I better be going. Thanks for the coffee, Albert. I sure needed it."

He stands up, "Sure, and sorry about the spill."

When I arrive home, the dogs are so glad to see me. They're wagging their tails. "Guess what, boys! We got Jeremy back!!!" They seem no more excited than they already were. I feed their little bellies and let them outside.

I gather an outfit for Jeremy. I pick out his favorite

sweats with his matching jacket and a blue t-shirt. I try to remember what shoes he had on. I grab his Skechers. This should do fine. I put it all in his gym bag.

My phone rings, and it's Rose. "I heard from Sandy, Alicia's mom, what happened to Jeremy?"

"How did she know?"

"Apparently, your mom got a hold of her to find out how she was doing and had a long conversation with her." Rose gets quiet and asks, "How come you didn't call me?"

I tell her, "It all happened so fast. On the upside, my Jeremy is back to himself!"

"What?! That's great!"

"Well, I hate to cut it short Rose, but I need to get back to the hospital. They're going to keep him overnight and run some tests, just to be sure he's okay."

I click end on the phone, let the dogs back in, grab the duffel bag, and make my way to the Prius. I think all this driving is helping me to keep my sanity. I think about the move, the wedding, having a baby... Jeremy is back!

When I walk into the hospital room, Albert is there. That comes as a surprise. I just seen him not long ago. Jeremy says, "Ah, look who's here, Cassie."

"I see that." I put his duffel bag between the sink counter and the tall cabinet.

Albert puts both his hands in his pockets, "I was here getting some tests." He points at his head, reminding us both of his tumor, "I thought I'd swing by to see how Jeremy is."

I say, "That was nice of you." I look over at Jeremy, who is sitting on his hospital bed. "Did they say what time tomorrow they're releasing you?"

He answers, "Depends on the test results."

Albert says, "Well, I better be going. It was nice talking with both of you, though under unfortunate circumstances."

Jeremy and I look at each other, then back at Albert, "It was nice talking to you too."

As soon as Albert leaves, I explain to Jeremy, "I just saw him at the Coffee Brewery. I thought it was strange to see him so much there, but then he pointed out that he lives above it."

Jeremy lies back down, "Ah. That makes sense."

I take his hand in mine, "Do you want me to spend the night here with you?"

"No, you need to get back and take care of the dogs. I'll be fine. It's only one night, and I'm fairly sure they'll be releasing me in the morning."

I take a seat on the recliner next to his bed. A few nurses walk in and tell me they're going to take him for an MRI. I watch them prep Jeremy, then see him take a seat on the wheelchair. "I'll be here when you get back." I smile.

The nurse says, "It may take a while because right after this one they're doing some more tests."

Jeremy looks at me, "Why don't you go down to the cafeteria and get yourself something to eat."

I nod my head in agreement, "Sounds good to me."

As I walk to the cafeteria, I'm feeling somewhat empty inside. Don't get me wrong! I'm ecstatic to have Jeremy back. It just feels like everything has caught up to me at once. The realization that I had lost Jeremy, Alicia still not found.

I look around the room, and I don't recognize anyone, not even a nurse. I order a grilled chicken sandwich and some fries. After I pay, I walk through to another wide, open room. I load up on ketchup for the fries and find a small, round table to sit at. There are a few people sitting by themselves. I'm just not used to it. I'm either home and eating on the couch, with clients, or with Jeremy. I never sit alone in public and eat by myself. It feels strange.

When I'm finished eating, I look at my watch and wonder if Jeremy is back yet. It's been about an hour. I make my way back up, stopping in the gift shop. I look around, wasting time. I'd get Jeremy another plant, but neither of us have green thumbs, so I'll be lucky if the first one survives. I find a few crossword puzzle books and decide to purchase them. "Do you have pens or pencils?"

She points at a shelf next to the candy. "Right," She reaches over, "here."

I walk into Jeremy's room and hold up the books, "Look what I bought!" I hand him one along with an ink pen. "How are you feeling?"

He answers, "This might seem weird, I'm mentally exhausted and physically restless." He opens his book to the first crossword puzzle. "On the good side, I'm done with tests. That makes me happy, they're draining."

I walk over to him and give him a kiss on his forehead, "I'm just glad you're back to your old self. I was starting to worry you wouldn't get your memory back."

"Yeah, it was like a mental block. It's the strangest thing I've ever felt or dealt with. Well, besides your mood swings."

I playfully hit him on the shoulder with my book, "Hey now."

Chapter 44

I'm on my way to the hospital this morning. Coffee is in the cup holder, keys in the ignition, and eyes on the road. I'm meeting Jeremy at the entry door. I can't wait for our life to get back to normal. A routine I realize I miss and need.

I pull up, and a nurse wheels Jeremy to the passenger side. I ask him, "You can't walk?"

He laughs and says, "They insisted." He rubs his beard that he needs to shave, "Talk about feeling helpless."

On the drive home I ask him, "Do you want to stop at the Brewery for a coffee?"

"No, I just want to get back home. I feel gritty and nasty. It'll be nice to have a long shower. Want to join me?"

I raise an eyebrow, "Feeling nasty both ways, huh?" We both laugh.

When we get home the dogs are overzealous to see Jeremy. It's as if they know he's returned to his old self. He gives them kisses and hugs. Then, he lets them out back to play. He says, "Maybe I should join them before I shower."

"Babe, I wouldn't push yourself right after staying in the hospital. Sounds like a bit much. Not to sound like a worry wart."

He closes the back door, "Nah, you're probably right."

While he takes his shower, I make us a late breakfast of pork chops and eggs. Jeremy's favorite! I put on some coffee, then set the table. By the time I'm pouring us both an orange juice, he's finished. I tell him, "That was fast."

"Well, you didn't join me." He winks at me.

"I figured you were starving after all that bland hospital food."

He says, "It actually wasn't too bad."

I make our plates, "I closed on the Donahue estate."

"I know you did! That's great, Cassie."

We both take a seat at the table, "Oh yeah, I forget you remember what happened while you didn't know what happened."

As he cuts his food up, he asks, "Strange, isn't it?"

"Do you remember running the stop sign? Lucky for us, Albert isn't going to press any charges."

Jeremy tilts his head with the most confused look on his face, "I didn't run a stop sign. He did."

"Are you sure about that babe? I spoke with Albert, and he was insistent that it was you."

Jeremy explains, "There's not even a stop sign where I passed through. He had the stop sign. You know where Old Mills Road is. There's no stop sign for me there."

As I'm cutting up my pork chop, I ask Jeremy, "Why do you think he lied?"

With his mouth full, Jeremy says, "Maybe he's still in some shock too. I mean, he does have a brain tumor. Maybe he's not thinking straight."

I'm hesitant, "Yeah, maybe."

When we are finished with dinner, we go relax on the couch. Both of us are snuggled in the same cover. We're flipping through the channels. "I don't really see anything I want to watch. Do you?"

He finds a movie about a serial killer on the run. They have his name but not his location. "I think this looks interesting."

I laugh and say, "It's a good thing you're sitting here with me, or I'd never be able to watch stuff like this." I get quiet and then add, "What if I have nightmares tonight?"

He answers, "You'll be glad to open your eyes and see your hero to the right of you, just waiting to save you from your dark hours." He shifts the couch pillow behind his back, "Do you want to go to the house tomorrow and see what else needs to be done?"

"Yeah, I'd love to!" I kiss his cheek and put my head on his shoulder.

Chapter 45

I'm so infuriated, to the point my hands are shaking. Not only is Jeremy still alive, but now he has his memory back. I think of ideas to get rid of him once and for all. Nothing I think of seems logical. I brainstorm, as I sit waiting for the coffee to brew. The drip is so slow, I start to feel impatient. Maybe if I go downstairs and order a coffee I'll get inspired, as I people watch. Yeah, that's what I'll do!

I make my way downstairs and walk up to the counter. There's a gal there with a name tag that says Alice. She asks if she can help me.

"I'll take a tall, black coffee." After I pay, I just stand there, waiting for her to make change for me. Afterward, I go to the other end of the counter and wait for them to call my name. I scope the room for a table I can sit at that will be easy to see other individuals from. I spot one and put my keys on it before someone else snatches it up. Then, I go to retrieve my coffee.

As I make myself comfortable, a short blonde walks in. She's a sight for sore eyes. Big hair, big boobs, and a big butt. That's a combination that sounds nice, especially tonight. Too bad I'm already taken. She has no idea what she's missing out on. What if I set a trap? What if I were to hire a blonde like herself, to make the moves on Jeremy and lure him to a hotel? All while I take pictures and send them to Cassie, anonymously. Where would I do that? I never see Jeremy go out. All he does is work and spend time with Cassie. Bad idea!

I can't cause a car wreck again. It would be too obvious. Maybe I need some more time to watch him and get to know his routine a little better. The thought of following him to work every day and then back home, is too much. I already know what he does. That's not going to work either. I'm so frustrated. I slam my hand against the tabletop, causing everyone to stop what they're doing and stare at me. For reflex's sake I say, "Ouch," and make it look as if it was an accident, as I stand up.

I decide maybe sleeping on it would be the best solution. Maybe I could watch Crime Stoppers or CSI. Maybe they'll give me some ideas to invest in. For now, I'm going to put it to rest. I decide to go back to Cassie's property line, behind her bedroom and spy. She never closes her curtains. I guess having a house backed to the woods, she feels she doesn't need to. Maybe she secretly hopes I'm watching.

I pull up a mile down the road and hike my way to her. I get to the tree line and find a stump to sit on. It's almost as if it was made for me. I need to bring some binoculars, but this view will have to do for now. It's hard to see in the windows during the day. Two vehicles are parked outside, so I know she's home. It should be my vehicle next to hers. I know that's the way she really wants it. I look at my watch, realizing it's too early to stay until dark. So, I hike my way back to my car and leave.

I arrive at my apartment, mentally drained. I guess from thinking of ways to eliminate Jeremy from Cassie's world. There's not room for both of us. At least my hands aren't shaking now. It's just too bad I couldn't see Cassie. I miss her. I guess it's not fair leaving her to miss me. She probably feels neglected. "Soon, my Cassie, soon."

A nap later, and I'm feeling back to my old self. My hands are steady, and my stamina is up. I pay a little visit to Cassie's house again. I park in the same place I did earlier. This time, I brought binoculars and a flashlight.

I make my way to the small trail that my visits are starting to form. I find the tree stump and wait for the sun to finish going down. Once it does, I pull out my binoculars from its case. I look to the bedroom, but the lights are off. I skim my way to the kitchen and notice a small light on. "Come on Cassie, I want to see you. I need to see you."

Right about the time I say that, the dogs are let outside. I'm especially quiet now. I don't want to alert them, where they start barking toward me, notifying anyone I'm here. I end up making my way back through the trail. No sense staying there while the dogs are out. I get back in my car and go home.

I open my apartment door, taking it all in. I love this place. The freedom in which it stands for and the quietness. I'm the man of this domain. Yeah, I'm happy with it. I throw my keys on the breakfast counter and put on some lounge pants.

I turn the channels until I find 20/20. This should be good. A serial killer is on the loose. He finds look alike victims around the same age and height. I never really understood serial killers much. I don't understand why they go around murdering a bunch of people for satisfaction. My situation is different. I'm fighting for a woman I love, who loves me.

I get my phone and go on social media. I see she's on Facebook. I am able to save some pictures from her page and print them. She's beautiful. It's the smile she always gives me when she sees me. Genuine! I decide I'm going to buy a frame for this photo. Maybe not today, I'm already in my lounge pants, but definitely tomorrow. As I'm scrolling through, I find another photo of her I like a lot. I can frame one and put it on my nightstand. Where would I put the other? I guess I could hang it on my wall.

As the photo is printing, I hear a knock at my door. I get up surprised and walk to the door, peeking out the peephole. "Hello?" I see the hag with my kids. I say, "What the hell," as I open the door.

She comes straight in, with the two kids dragging behind her. "I know it's getting late, but I have to work tonight. Do you think you could watch the kids? It's a night shift, so I don't feel comfortable leaving them at home alone."

I ask, "Why didn't you just have Randy watch them?"

She sighs, rolling her eyes and answers, "He's not home. Which isn't unusual for him these days!"

I look at my two kids. They both look tired and confused. "Sure, I'll watch them." I lead the kids to their bedrooms. "Why didn't you call first?"

She says, "I debated leaving them home to sleep, but then my gut kept telling me something could go wrong. It was a last-minute decision."

I tell her, "And a good one at that."

I show her to the door, "Have a good night at work."

I decide that I'm not giving much money to the wife. The kids are almost grown. I can use some of the savings for a cabin in the woods. Maybe I can buy an old hunter's lodge. Somewhere kind of competitive to what Jeremy was doing for Cassie. I think I might hire her to find it for me. That'll give us more time together. It'll also buy me time to think about what to do with Jeremy.

Chapter 46

It's really bugging me that Albert Wilson lied about Jeremy running the stop sign. Maybe Albert thought he'd get in trouble with the law. Maybe since he said he wasn't going to press charges, he thought he'd put it in our heads not to press charges.

I'm digging through my drawers. I'm trying to find my black negligee. Lately, I've been missing clothes. It's odd because I'm sure I saw my hoodie in the closet a few days ago. I can't find it anywhere. Also, I'm missing a pair of panties that match my bra. Now, it's my nightie. What the hell is going on? I yell toward the living room, "Have you seen my black negligee? You know, the one that's your favorite?"

"Only on you, babe." He shouts back. I'm in no mood for humor. This is just getting weird. I know he hasn't cheated on me because he literally hasn't been himself. So where are my clothes going? And why? I rub my face... I'll check the laundry one more time. I know it's not in there, but where the hell could they be?!

I check the laundry with no avail. Maybe I'll have a talk with Jeremy. Maybe this stuff came up missing before he had amnesia. Maybe he is having an affair on me. Oh my God, all these maybes. I walk into the living room and have a seat on the couch, next to Jeremy. "Honey, is there something you're not telling me?"

He looks at me with a puzzled face and asks, "What do you mean?"

"We're the only ones in this house. I'm missing my

panties, my hoodie, and now my black negligee. It's getting kind of creepy." I'm staring him down to see if there's even a hint of him inviting a woman into our house. Maybe he's giving them to her at her house.

He asks, "Are you suggesting something? Look, I've had amnesia. I've been going out of my mind, but I haven't been taking your personal belongings. That would be weird." His expression changes to annoyed.

"Sorry, I had to ask. I mean where else could they be going?"

He looks at me funny, "Did you check the laundry?"

I roll my eyes, "Of course, I did. I wouldn't have been asking you twenty questions if I hadn't."

He scratches his head, "Well, excuse me for asking."

I let out a sigh, "I'm sorry if I sound bothered. It's just kind of scary. If you didn't take them and I can't find them... then who's taking my stuff?"

He lets out a nervous laugh, "Come on honey, you'll find them. I'm sure they're just misplaced."

I get a creepy feeling, but I keep it to myself. I'm glad he thinks this is funny because I sure in the hell not laughing, but maybe he can't be trusted. I raise an eyebrow in suspicion, as I look him over.

He suddenly stares in my direction and asks, "What are you giving me that look for? I promise you, I didn't do anything with your clothes. What do you think I could possibly do with them?"

Should I say it? That he could have been having an affair before his concussion, or should I just keep it to myself? I don't want to sound like a jealous lunatic who's insecure about myself. I'm neither of those things. I just can't figure out where my stuff is going.

I decide to leave well enough alone. Maybe he's right. I'll find my belongings somewhere in the house. I just don't know where else to look. I let go of my frustration and regain my composure. I rest my head on Jeremy's shoulder. "So much has happened. They still haven't found Alicia. I'm beginning to wonder if they ever will."

He kisses the top of my head, "I know, honey. They'll find her." He then adds, "Did they ever check into the credit card receipts?"

"I don't know. I'll call Sandy in the morning and find out what she knows. I'm sure if they've found something on the receipts, they'll notify her."

The wrinkle in the middle of his eyebrows, furrows in deeper, "I'm as concerned, Cassie. If it doesn't seem like it... it's only because I have so much on my mind." He gives me a quick kiss, "I don't mean to seem so cold."

I curl up against him, "I know, babe."

Chapter 47

The next morning, I jump straight out of bed, pour myself some coffee, and call Sandy. "Hey, it's me, Cassie."

She responds, "Oh Cassie, hi sugar. How are you?"

"I'm holding up the best I can, all things considered. How are you?"

She clears her throat. I'm not sure if it's to cover up the tears in her voice or stalling for time to figure it out. "I'm a mess, but I'm trying to stay strong for Alicia's sake. The last thing she needs is to come home and find out I've had a heart attack or become ill."

I pause, wondering if my asking questions could cause her to be either of the two. "Sandy, have you heard any more information about her?"

She is quiet for a moment, then says, "No, not really."

"Did they get the receipts from the jewelry store? I know that was mentioned."

She says, "I'm not supposed to talk about the case. You didn't hear this from me, but yeah, they got the receipts. That's all I know, though."

I bite my lip, "I wonder what's taking them so long."

She answers, "Well, it is an ongoing investigation. Without her whereabouts, they don't know what to think. And I'm pretty sure the officers had to hand the case over to the detectives."

A long pause then Jeremy walks in and says something, but I'm so concentrated on the phone call that I have no idea what he said. "Well, I guess I better get ready for work.

Thanks a lot, Sandy."

I look over to Jeremy. "What did you say?"

He tells me, "I was basically talking to myself out loud. Sorry, I hope I didn't disrupt your phone call."

"No, you didn't. I found out what I needed to know, and after that it was kind of awkward." I go into the bedroom and start changing out of my pajamas. I yell in, "The police have the receipts from the jewelry store."

He yells back, "Were they of any use?"

I slip on my heels, "She doesn't know. I guess they haven't finished looking through them. She said she's not really supposed to be talking about the case with anyone."

He hands me my keys. I ask, "Are you going into work today?"

He smiles ear to ear, "Yes, thank God! I'm ready for it."

"Are you going to stop by our place?"

"Not without you. Do you want to meet there later? We can make sure everything is like we want it. There's really no more decisions that need to be made that we haven't already decided on."

"What about the washer and dryer?"

He says, "I did that last night. I hope you don't mind. I just got the whirlpool stand-ups. Big enough to hold our queen size comforter."

I give him a quick kiss, "Sounds perfect."

I make my way to the office. The drive is healing for me. It's like resting from everything that has happened over the past few weeks. As I walk in, Marge asks, "How's everything at home?"

"Fine," I'm relieved to finally say. I'm so relieved. I feel my shoulders slinking slowly down from being all tensed up.

The phone rings. I call out, "I'll get it!"

"Hello?"

"Hi. This is Mrs. Thelma Rosenberg. We are planning to move when the kids are out of school this summer. It's approaching fast! I'm wondering if you would be able to help?"

Oh, how exciting! "Would you be selling your house or just buying?"

She responds, "Well, we plan on renting this one to my niece. We have this one all squared away. We're concentrated on buying."

"Sure, I can help! There are a lot of great places on the market right now. Would you like to make an appointment to tell me what it is you're looking for?"

I can hear the happiness in her tone, "I sure would! How does Saturday look for you?"

"Saturday will be just fine. What time?"

She replies, "I guess one o'clock, by then my husband and I will have had our lunch."

I get a piece of paper and jot it down, as I recite it. "Great! I'll see you Saturday, at one o'clock."

I look over at Marge and smile, "I'm glad I answered that phone call, and you didn't." I playfully stick my tongue out at her.

She says, "Hey now, I see how you are." We are both giddy from getting another possible house sale. Business has been great as of lately. It's keeping me too busy to sit and continuously fret over things I can't control.

I get on the computer and start going through the house listings. I update the website to say sold on a few of them. After, I look out the window and see Albert Wilson sitting at a table outside of the Coffee Brewery. I debate going straight over there and asking him why he lied to me, but I've never been good at confrontation. I think of other ways I could bring it up. Before I know it, I'm making my way across the street. I walk past, as if I don't see him. Then I hear, "Cassie?"

I turn my head and say, "Oh, hi Albert. How are you?"

He says, "The kids had a day off school for parent teacher conferences, so their mom dropped them at my place yesterday. I didn't sleep very well and decided to come down here to have some coffee."

How could a dad possibly lie about a stop sign? It just doesn't make sense. I still try to conjure a way to bring it up. I can't think of anything that would make sense in the conversation. "Sounds like you're pretty busy."

He says, "Why don't you grab a cup of coffee and join me!"

I think about the stop sign again. I reply, "Okay."

After I get my coffee, I go back outside and join Albert. "It's such a pretty day." I take a seat across from him, not next to him. I notice how attractive he is and wonder why he's not with his wife. I ask him, "So, what's been keeping you awake?"

He rubs his coffee handle, "I'm going through a divorce."

"Oh no! I'm so sorry to hear that. If I'm being too inquisitive just let me know."

He says, "No, no, no. You're not being too inquisitive. If I'm being honest, it feels good to talk about it."

I take a sip of my coffee and ask, "What prompted the divorce?"

He sighs and says, "We have outgrown one another."

I hear Marge call my name from across the street. I look over at her and lean in toward the direction she's in. She's telling me to grab her a coffee too. It's probably for the best that I don't confront Albert anyway. He is suffering from a brain tumor. Maybe he just doesn't remember it right. "Well, it was nice talking to you Albert, but I'm going to get Marge's coffee now."

He holds up his cup, "Until we meet again."

I bring Marge her coffee and go into my office. I work on catching up on paperwork. By the time I'm done, three hours have passed. I grab my keys and head toward the door. "See you tomorrow."

I call Jeremy, "Hi, honey! Are you at our new place?"

He says, "Yeah."

"Okay, I'm on my way."

Chapter 48

Wow, that was some luck. I only went to sit outside because I saw her car there. Good thing I did too! It's nice to have coffee with the love of my life. I saw the way she was looking me over. She definitely wants me. Too bad that, quote Cassie, "Marge" got in the way. I think Cassie would have stayed longer if not for her disturbance. Maybe I should do something about her too!

I go back upstairs to my apartment and make the kids some breakfast before they wake up. Just a simple eggs and bacon, with some toast. Joey comes in first, "It sure smells good in here, Dad."

"Hey, you called me Dad this time."

"Yeah, Randy has really been on me about it. He's right, I have some growing up to do."

Maggie not long after, follows in. "You grow up?? I highly doubt that."

I say, "Maggie, be nice to your brother," as I make each of their plates. I'm so full from the coffee, I can't eat.

I look at my watch. "It's almost time to drive you home."

Joey looks disappointed, "Oh Dad, can't we stay for the day and go do something?"

I answer, "Your mom's instructions, son."

After I get the kids home, I come back to the apartment to decide what I'm going to do about the woman "Marge" and Jeremy. I can't stand Marge. I finally had an opportunity to spend time with my woman and she interrupts. How dare her! I'll teach her a lesson.

She's the Prey, He's the Stalker

As the day turns to night, I watch out my apartment window to see what time Marge leaves the office. I decide to get in my car and wait. This way, I can follow her home to see where she lives. Finally, she comes out at about nine o'clock. I tail her. She doesn't live that far away. I'd say four or five blocks before she's pulling in a suburbia home. I take a few photos of her going inside her house. I never have them developed. I just keep them in the camera until I transfer them to my computer.

I'm feeling in a good mood, now that I have some structure as to what I'm going to do. I stop in a fast-food joint and order from the window. "Yeah, I'll take a burger and fries."

By the time I roll out, I'm tired. I'm ready to get home, eat, and go to bed. Tomorrow's a big day. I'll take care of Marge then. Once I get home, I take my food to bed. I flip through the television stations until I find an old black and white movie that captures my attention.

When I wake up, I'm happy. I'm looking forward to paying Marge a little visit. I look out my living room window to see her car in front of the real estate office. Perfect! I have her right where I want her. I go downstairs and order myself a coffee. "Black, please."

After I get my coffee, I make my way upstairs and sit at the table in front of the bay window, overlooking the stage and real estate office. I take note that Cassie's Prius isn't there. She must be showing houses today. My hard-working little woman.

When night comes, I wait by the alley until Marge comes out. Then, I leave my car parked in front with the hood up, as if I'm having problems with my vehicle. She says, "Do you need any help sir?"

"Actually, I do. If you could just start my car for me, while I screw this in..."

By the time she gets in my car, I've already strangled her. She made it extremely easy for me. I tell her dead body, "You won't be in our way now." I take her to the same place I disposed of Alicia's body. "Now you have a friend."

    I don't even remember driving home. It's like my reflexes took me here. I take a shower and put on some pajamas. It's been a long, fulfilling day. Next on my list, Jeremy.

Chapter 49

I walk back into the house. "Jeremy, you're not going to believe this. I went in to work and Marge wasn't there. She's always there. I tried calling her cell phone numerous times and didn't get an answer."

He says, "Weird, maybe it's some kind of emergency. Maybe it's family or vehicle related. She could have broken down and had to be towed."

"That doesn't explain why she wouldn't answer her phone. She always picks up. No, this isn't her usual self. What's even stranger, is her SUV is at the office." A chill runs up and down my arm. I know Marge. This isn't like her at all!

I look in my phone book for her home number. Maybe her husband can answer some questions for me. Oh, here it is. I lift the book closer to my eyes and dial the number. "Hello, this is Cassie. Is this John?"

The voice on the other end of the line responds, "Yes, this is John."

"I've been trying to get a hold of Marge. The office isn't opened, and I saw her SUV there."

He sighs and says, "She didn't come home last night. I have to wait twenty-four hours to file a missing person's report. I've already called everyone I can." He sounds frantic.

I ask, "Do you want me and Jeremy to come over?"

He sniffles and says, "Sure, we can brainstorm other possibilities of where she might have gone or be at."

"Okay, give me about thirty minutes."

"Jeremy, babe. John, Marge's husband, wants us to come over and go over possibilities that he may not have thought of."

He comes walking in and wraps his arm around me. He gives me a kiss on the cheek, "Sure, honey." He grabs his shoes and takes a seat on the kitchen chair. "Do you think she could be having an affair?"

I ask, "Marge? No way. She's crazy about John."

As he's tying his last shoe up, he says, "Well, it's the only thing that makes any logical sense. Maybe she was having an affair and fell asleep." He gets quiet. He then adds, "Maybe her car is there because her lover picked her up."

"No, no. I'm telling you Marge wouldn't cheat on John. She's just not that way." I grab my keys. I can't help wondering if he's thinking like that, because he was secretly having an affair on me. "She's crazy in love with him. He's all she talks about."

As we walk out, "I've heard of stranger happenings."

We get in my Prius. I drive fast because one... I want to get there, and two... my mind is going a mile a minute. "I'm telling you, she's not cheating on him and never would. Something is seriously wrong."

"You could be paranoid because Alicia hasn't turned up yet."

"No, but it's true, that makes me even more worried about Marge. It's like we have a killer on the loose."

He leans his chair back a little more, "Alicia has been gone a long time without any word. Marge though, she hasn't been missing that long. What, since yesterday?"

I correct him, "Last night. John said they won't let him file a missing person's report yet."

"Can't they just track her phone?"

I answer, "I'm not sure how far they've gone. I'll find out more information once we're there."

I pull into her suburban home driveway. She lives pretty

close to the office. It's probably close enough that she could take a walk if she wanted to. I knock on the door. "John, it's us. We're here."

He opens the door, "Come in."

We walk through the entry hall into the living room and take a seat on her couch. John sits on the oversized chair. Marge has the living room decorated in sunflowers, even though it's summer. "Any news?" I ask.

John gets up, walks to the table, and pulls a book off it. He then walks over to me, and he hands it to me. "I've been through every number in her phone book. Do you have any suggestions beyond it?"

I flip through the pages, reading all the names. It takes me a little bit. Afterward, I tell him, "No. Everyone we mutually know is in here."

"Do you have another car she may have taken?"

John shakes his head no. "Something's not right." He takes the phone book back from me. He sets it on the coffee table. "Has she mentioned... another man?"

Odd, I can tell he was thinking the same thing Jeremy was, but I know better! He says, "No, no. Marge wouldn't do that to you. You're right, something's wrong."

Jeremy asks, "Did the police trace her phone?"

"I don't believe they do anything until twenty-four hours have passed." John stands up. "Can I make you something to drink? I have coffee, juices, and pops."

"I would love a coffee."

Jeremy adds in, "I'll take a coffee too, thanks."

I look at Jeremy, who raises his eyebrow. "See, even he thinks there's another man involved."

"I'm telling you Jeremy, there's no other man."

John walks in with our coffees. I stand up and retrieve mine, while he hands the other to Jeremy. "Did they say a specific time?"

"Well, she gets off work at five, so that's when I'm going to the police station and filing one."

Jeremy looks at his smart watch, "It's thirty minutes 'til then."

"Yeah, I should be going. I didn't realize it was this late."

I'm sure the man isn't thinking right. He has no idea where his wife is and why she didn't come home. To top it off, he's questioning her commitment to him. I guess it's better than thinking the worst-case scenarios, that's what's been running through my head.

"Where would you like us to put our coffee cups?"

John says, "You can just leave them on the coffee table."

Chapter 50

It was a long night. I tossed and turned. I don't think I fell asleep until about three this morning. By the time I wake up, it's eleven o'clock. Jeremy is lying next to me. I hit him with a pillow, "Baby, we have to get up." I point to the radio clock next to him.

He runs his hand through his hair, "It's eleven already. I feel like I just closed my eyes."

"Yeah, me too." I get up from bed. "I'll make us some coffee."

When Jeremy walks into the kitchen, I tell him, "I'm not sure what to do. I'm supposed to meet with Mrs. Rosenberg on Saturday, at one. All her information is in the office, and I don't have a key for it. Marge isn't answering, and for that matter, can't even be found. I'll call John. Maybe she's back home."

"Hi, John! This is Cassie. I'm calling to find out if Marge came home?"

"No, she did not. I filed the missing person's report, and I called all the local hospitals again, for the second time."

"I hate to ask you this, but I'm supposed to be meeting some of her clients Saturday. I have no way of knowing their information to call them. It's all on my desk. Do you have a spare key to the office?"

"She has a bunch of keys in her desk drawer. Does one go to the office? I don't know. You'd have to try them, but fair warning, there are five of them." He coughs, "And like I said, I'm not even sure if any of the five go to the office."

"That's fine. I'll be by to pick them up later."

I pour Jeremy a cup of coffee and hand it to him with a hug. "Have I told you lately that I love you?"

He takes a drink and smiles at me, "I love you too. So, what's the word on Marge?"

"He's tried the hospitals and filed the report. Still no word from her. Do you think this is linked with Alicia?"

Jeremy stands right next to me and puts an arm around my shoulder, "If you keep talking like that, I'm not going to let you go to work." He looks at his watch, "Oh shit, speaking of..." He sets his coffee down and speed walks to the bedroom. I figure he's getting dressed. He must be running late.

I let the dogs out, finish my coffee, and go into the bedroom to get dressed, as Jeremy is leaving. He gives me a kiss on the forehead. "See you tonight."

I say, "Have a good day at work." I wonder if it's just work he's going to. If one more of my clothes goes missing there is going to be some serious consequences.

It's almost two in the afternoon by the time I get to John and Marge's house. I don't even have to knock. John must have been standing by the window so he could see me coming. "Hi." He hands me the keys. "Good luck with that."

"Do you not have work today? I didn't mean to hold you up if you do."

John says, "Oh, I'm retired."

I take the keys and head to the office. The traffic is crazy for just being a few blocks away. I try not to tailgate, but the person behind me is... which makes it impossible not to. I honk my horn at the person behind me, but the person in front of me thinks I'm honking at her. She turns around and gives me the finger.

I'm glad to get to the office. That was crazy! I get to the door and try all the keys. None of them work. I let out a disappointed sigh. I walk across the street to get a coffee. "Black smoke, please." I'm the only one in line. She doesn't even bother taking my name. She just pours me some and hands me the cup. "Thanks."

I remember that I left the dogs outside and decide I better get back home. Otherwise, they'll have no water. I quickly walk to my car, without any hassles. My phone rings.

"Hey, baby," Jeremy's voice says, on the other end. "Any news on Marge?"

"Nothing new, and none of the keys work at the office. I'm not sure what to do. I guess we'll probably lose Mrs. Rosenberg. I should have given her my cell phone, but she was still fresh on the list."

By the time Jeremy and I are off the phone, I'm back home. I unlock the door and let the dogs back in. I make sure they have fresh water and call John back. I get the answering machine. "Hi, John. It's me, Cassie. None of the keys worked. Just give me a call, and we'll work out a time for me to bring them back to you tomorrow."

I go to the backyard and play with the dogs for a while. When we get back inside, I feed them. After, I find my couch cover and relax until Jeremy gets home. I don't really feel like cooking, so I call him. "Do you think you can pick up a pizza tonight? I'm in the mood for one."

I flip through the channels. Nothing. I pick up a book, but before I'm done with a chapter, I'm asleep. "Run, run for your life. I'm running as fast as I can. I'm amongst a crowd, that if I'm not fast enough, will trample right over me."

"Wake up, Cassie." Jeremy is leaning over me. I feel sweat all over my face. "I just had the worst nightmare." I begin telling him about it. "It felt so real."

He explains, "But the main thing is, it wasn't real. You're going to be fine, Cassie."

He flops down at the end of the couch and puts my feet in his lap. He takes off my shoes and begins massaging my feet. "I know there's been a lot going on lately. You're missing two of your dear friends. In the end, I'm sure it'll work out. I'm sure they'll be fine."

"Sure? You're sure? How can you say that, Jeremy?

You don't have any information. You don't have any idea." I feel short with him. Truth is, he's on my nerves with this 'so sure' attitude. And I'm not convinced he's not cheating on me.

"You're right, I'm sorry. I want you to feel better, Cassie. I need you to know you're okay."

I explain to him, "I'm not worried about me. I'm worried about Alicia and Marge."

"I just thought since you were having nightmares, maybe you are concerned about your safety too."

Maybe he's right. Maybe somewhere deep down I'm concerned about me. It wouldn't be unreasonable. I really haven't had too much time to think about it. When I'm home, all I want to do is sleep. When I wake up, I'm on the go.

Chapter 51

I'm watching the news. Alicia is on again. I'm surprised it didn't say anything about Marge's disappearance yet. I wonder if they are linking the two women. They still haven't found the bodies. That comes as no surprise to me.

I need to figure out what to do with Jeremy. With the office being closed, I haven't seen Cassie. I miss her, and I know she's missing me too. So, I need to do something with Jeremy sooner rather than later. I'm out of options, though. I certainly can't bring him back here to my apartment. I debate about buying a cabin in the woods again.

I have Cassie's phone number. It would be a good way to get closer to her. I could have her become my real estate broker for the cabin. I know she'd love it. Rose gave me her phone number. I could call it and say she was referred to me by Rose. Rose did say she might want insurance.

I decide to quickly dial her number before I change my mind. "Is this Cassie?"

"Yes, this is Cassie."

"This is Albert Wilson. I was referred to you by Rose. I'm interested in buying a cabin-like setting, surrounded by nature. Is this something you could help me with?"

She is quiet a moment, and then she responds, "Umm. Yes. I won't be in the office, but I'm sure I can work with you from home. Our website has a lot of listings, if you want to go through them and decide which ones you want to see. Then, we will figure out how to go about it when we get that far. My boss hasn't been in the office, and she's the only one with the keys. Right now, I'm working from home."

I think, as should be. She was in the way. "Great. When would be a good time for us to go over the listings?"

"Albert Wilson! I recognize your name now. You are the one that was in the crash with my husband, right? How do you know Rose?"

"Yes, that's me. I'm Rose's insurance agent."

"How about we meet at the coffee shop tomorrow at noon. We can get some lunch and talk about the listings you find of interest. That is, if you can go over them tonight?"

"Sure can. Thanks, Cassie. I'll see you tomorrow."

"Oh, Albert, if you have any questions about any of them, don't hesitate to call."

That conversation went better than expected. Now we have a date. This cabin will be the place I take Jeremy to, and of course, a place my kids can go to during the summer months when I have them. I'm so excited.

I fetch my laptop and find a comfortable spot. I decide on the table in front of the windows, overlooking the coffee shop. This way, I can search places and take periodic breaks to stare out at the tables. There are a lot of listings, but the search questions help to minimize them. I fill in all the information needed.   I think it's best to go with four bedrooms. It sounds kind of big for a cabin, but the kids each need their own room. I could get three, since Randy is getting older. One day he might stay here, or one day they'll inherit it for their own children. Yeah, I'm sticking with four.

I go through six or seven farm listings, when I get to this lodge that's on thirty acres. The land is surrounded by conservation, which makes the spread even bigger. It sounds like what I'm looking for too! It's a rustic cedar home with four bedrooms and three-and-a-half baths. I jot down the listing number. I don't really see anything else that captures my interest. I try to find a second home, but most are too new or still being occupied. I want a turnkey. The sooner I get to Jeremy, the better!

I decide I'm going to keep Jeremy around for a while before I strangle him. Yes, I have bigger plans for the man that thought he could have my woman. I will get the inside scoop about Cassie. The closer the sentiments, the better. I have a feeling Jeremy can help me with that. In fact, there's a lot about Cassie he can help me with.

I pick up the phone and call Cassie. "Hi, it's Albert. I only found one place I'm interested in, and this looks like it could be it."

"I looked up some too and found one. Give me your listing number."

I quickly give it to her, and it turns out we found the same place. It doesn't surprise me since we are supposed to be together. Naturally, we are in sync.

"Okay, I'll see you tomorrow at one."

The phone clicks. I look at my watch and realize it's my bedtime. I feel kind of stupid for calling her this late. I didn't realize it was almost eight o'clock. I shrug, as I make my way to the bedroom. Her voice is so sensual.

I kept waking up throughout the night, so by the time it's eight o'clock, I'm dreary. I search through the bedroom TV channels. Nothing looks good, so instead I go to the kitchen and make myself some coffee. When it's done, I take my mug to the table in front of the windows. I look out at the crowd coming in and out of the coffee shop.

I stretch and run my fingers through my hair. I wonder what I should wear. I think about a button-up dress shirt with jeans and cowboy boots. Yeah, that will do it. Nice, yet casual. I think she'll find me quite charming.

The hours drag by, but when one o'clock rolls around, I'm ready. I grab my keys and walk to the garage. My drive to her was fast. I'm in such a good mood. I can't wait to see her and this lodge.

Chapter 52

"Where are you going?" He gently grabs my arm and pulls me back into bed.

"I could only lie down for a nap, Jeremy." I look at the radio clock on his nightstand. "It's half-past twelve. I have to go and meet with Albert, to see a lodge."

"First, he crashes into me, then he steals away my woman. What's this man want from me?!" He kisses my hand and smiles.

"I love you, babe... but I gotta go." I rush, as I'm putting my clothes back on. I find my keys. "I'll see you later."

Jeremy doesn't work today. I normally keep my schedule clear to match his, but with Marge not at the office and Alicia missing... keeping busy is saving my sanity. I'm not sure how other people pull through, but this is my instinctive move.

I call Albert. "Hey, I'm running a few minutes late. If you want, you can go ahead and start checking out the grounds."

He answers, "It's okay. They have a porch swing out front. I'm currently sitting on it. I'm enjoying the view. Take your time, I'll be fine."

When I pull up, I see Albert is still sitting on the swing. I make my way up the porch. We shake hands. He holds onto mine a little longer than I'm comfortable with, so I pull it back. He says, "You look lovely today."

It's so nice to hear a compliment. I respond, "Thank you." Sometimes I think Jeremy has forgotten to say a sweet word or two about my looks.

I open the door, and we enter a log home. "Wow." It catches me by surprise because the inside is much bigger. "You'd think the pictures would have done it justice, but they don't."

He says, "You got that right." He makes his way through the living room and into the kitchen.

When we make our way upstairs, I notice there's a cord hanging, leading to an attic door. I wonder if we should go up there, but I don't mention it. I figure Albert sees it too, and if he wanted to, he'd suggest it. I've always found attic's a little creepy. I never go in them with my clients. They go alone.

"The bedrooms here are huge, which is nice for a change. Everywhere I've lived so far has had tiny bedrooms." He walks into the master suite. "Wow, tile and a walk-in shower."

He looks me up and down while he says it. I feel uncomfortable and very wanted at the same time! When was the last time Jeremy made me feel wanted? He did grab me back into bed this morning, though. That was definite want. As my mind wanders, Albert snaps me back to the now, instead of the then.

"Double sinks, I really won't need those, since I'm going through a divorce."

I reply, "You might meet a lady friend and be glad you have them."

"I'm getting too old for lady friends." He looks at himself in the mirror and rubs his freshly shaven, gray hair chin.

"I don't know about that. You're quite handsome, Albert. I'm sorry you're going through a divorce, but that doesn't mean your dating life is over. Maybe you'll meet someone or who knows... get back together with your wife."

He puts his hand on my shoulder, "Thank you for your kind words, but I'm never getting back with her. I feel like weights came off my shoulders since I moved out."

He leans in and kisses me. At first, I didn't pull back. I

should have, but something inside me was wanting him. I'm not sure why. I'm happy with Jeremy. Finally, I stop him. "We can't."

"Sorry, I was caught up in the moment, and you were there..."

I cut him off, "It's alright. It just can't happen again. I'm Jeremy's fiancé, and I'm quite happy, Albert."

"I'd like to take a closer look at the fireplace." He goes back into the bedroom. The fireplace goes up from the bottom floor. The bedroom has French doors he can open and walk out onto a terrace that overlooks the living room. I find it strange that it doesn't have stairs leading down, but it could be a possibility if he wanted it to. I feel relieved at the change of topic.

He says, "It's gas." He hesitates, "I was hoping for wood. Let's go back downstairs and check the living room one." I follow his lead.

He bends down and looks around for a switch.

I say, "I found the remote." I hand it to him.

He turns it on. It takes a few minutes for the flame to start. "It's gas as well." He looks around at the log walls, "With all the trees around here, you'd think it'd be wood-burning."

He turns it back off and hands the remote to me. I say, "Some like the pleasure of not having to cut wood or having it brought in. Gas can be a luxury."

"Yeah, that's true, but there's nothing like the smell of actual wood while it's burning. Definitely better than smelling propane."

We enter the kitchen. All the appliances are updated. I open the oven that is inside the wall. "Oh my gosh, what a back saver. I wish we had one of these." I put my finger on my lips, "I didn't think of it while we were building our home."

"Were?" He walks over and stands behind me, as he checks out the oven. "Does that mean you're not anymore?"

"Were, because we're done now." I smile. "It's built. It's just waiting for us to move in."

"When do you plan to do that?"

I reply, "Soon, very soon."

During the ride home, I kept thinking about the kiss with Albert. Why did I feel all those emotions stir up? I want... wanted him. How could I do that to Jeremy?! I guess all of Albert's compliments played on my feelings.

Chapter 53

The next morning, Jeremy and I sleep in late, that is, until my phone rings. "Hello?"

"Cassie, it's Albert. I decided I want the lodge. I'd like to put an offer in."

"Hold on," I sit up and rub my eyes. As I make my way to the kitchen to grab something to write with, I almost trip over the dogs. I dig through the junk drawer until I find a halfway decent pen. "Okay," I say as I grab a tablet. "I'm ready."

I take down the information and make my way back to the bedroom. With Marge not in the office, I'm not sure what the best way to go through with this is. That's when I decide to co-op with another real estate agent. I can trust Danica. Even though she works for a company a town over, she basically runs the place. I give her a call. "Danica, it's me, Cassie Jennings. When you get this message will you please give me a call back."

It only took a few minutes before my phone rings. "Hey, Cassie. This is Danica. What's up?"

I tell her all about Marge missing. The situation of how I can't get into the office, and how I have a buyer that wants to make a bid! I tell her the whole giant mess I'm in. Danica tells me she'll handle it, and we can split the commission. I know Marge would be fine with her because they've been friends for years.

After I'm off the phone with her, I snuggle back in with Jeremy. I'm feeling a great relief. I wasn't sure what to do when Albert wanted to make a bid, but thanks to Danica, it's all taken care of. I gave her all Albert's information over the phone. It's just dotting the i's and crossing the t's now.

"I made a sale today. Danica and I are going to split the commission." I rub Jeremy's back, and then kiss where my fingers had traced.

He stretches out, "Sounds like a plan." He then adds, "It's been a long time since we've seen Danica. Why don't you invite her over to dinner?"

"Yeah, maybe after the sale." Then I say, "Of course, she'll probably want to go out and celebrate."

He answers, "That's okay too."

"Yeah, it's been a while since I've been out on the town. The more I think about it, the more it sounds like fun." I relax a bit. "Why don't you come with us?"

"Honey, you don't even know if you're going yet. Even if you do, I don't want to go." He puts his hand on the back of his head. "The bar scene just isn't me."

"Ughh, I thought dancing would be a nice distraction, though. Don't be a party pooper."

He laughs, "I'm not a party pooper. I'm just not a parti-er."

"Okay, okay, okay. I'll stop bugging you about it."

When we finally get out of bed, it's to let the dogs out while the coffee is brewing. We make ourselves comfortable on the couch. He asks, "So, you have another closing?"

I put my head in his lap, "I hope so. I'm hoping to get it done before we start packing to move."

Jeremy says, "We should already be packing. So, that's hardly fair."

"Maybe we should hire Three Men and a Truck. They'll do the packing for us." I look their number up on my phone, then put it in front of Jeremy's face. "See?"

"I'm not sure I'm comfortable with strangers packing up all of our stuff." He gets quiet, and I can tell he's thinking it out. "I guess it would be nice to have them load and unload the boxes."

I explain, "They don't just unload... if the boxes are labeled, they put them in the corresponding rooms."

Jeremy smiles, "That's even better." He runs his fingers through my hair. "What do you want to do today?"

"I'm okay with just lounging around here. How about later we go out back and play with the dogs? They've been cooped up all week without us." I close my eyes, and he leans down and kisses me.

He then says, "Okay, that's fine."

I dial up the moving company and they agreed to come Monday to give us a bid. When I get off the phone, I look up at Jeremy. "They'll need a moving date."

He responds, "Let's make it for the following Monday."

"Oh my god, do you think I can get everything packed by then?"

He rubs his chin, "We can do things slowly, Cass. It's not like we're in a hurry to get rid of this house."

"Yeah, I guess you're right. I'm not sure why I'm getting myself all wound up. I'm not used to taking my time on anything. I guess I'm just used to the hustle and bustle."

An hour later, we get off the couch and make our way to the backyard with the dogs. We play chase, fetch, hide and seek, and wear ourselves out, even more so than the dogs. "I can't do anymore, Cass. My legs are going to give out." Jeremy falls to the ground.

I fall next to him and laugh. "Yeah, me either." The three dogs circle us, with their tongues hanging out. "I guess I'm going to have to muster up the energy to go inside and get them some fresh water. Look at them with their tongues hanging out. Hahaha."

Jeremy stands up first and reaches his arm out toward me, which I gladly take his hand in mine, as he pulls me up. "I guess soon I'm going to need one of those - help, I've fallen, and I can't get back up - buttons."

He says, "You're much too young for that."

"By the time we're done packing, I doubt I'll feel that way."

He twirls a lock of my hair on his finger. "It's nice, knowing I have someone to grow old with."

"Yeah, I guess I've never looked at it that way." I start thinking of how he'll look when he's older. I accidentally laugh out loud, without realizing it, until it's too late.

"What are you laughing about?"

"I just saw you as a bald, old man, shrinking in height, and waving your cane at me."

He hits me with a couch pillow. "That's not funny."

Chapter 54

Today, I'm waiting to see if they accepted my offer on the lodge and my terms on moving in as soon as the inspection is done. After the kiss a few days ago, I realize I need to take care of Jeremy sooner rather than later. I could feel the want in Cassie, as she kissed me back. She definitely wanted more. The only one stopping her is Jeremy. She didn't say she didn't want to kiss me. She just introduced herself as his fiancé. As if guilt had played a role. Yes, I can take care of him. I check my voicemail. Damn, still no response from Cassie.

I walk nervously around my kitchen. Maybe I should call her. Right as I thought that, my phone rings. I hurry to it and answer. "Hello?"

"Albert?"

"This is he."

"This is Cassie. I have wonderful news. They accepted your offer."

"How soon can we get the inspection done?"

"I can get him out there on Wednesday. Is that soon enough for you?"

I feel relief and happiness set in, "Yes, yes. It's soon enough."

When I get off the phone with Cassie, I notice she didn't mention anything about the kiss. I know she's still thinking about it, though. From the tone of her voice, she's as excited about the lodge as I am. Hopefully, it's somewhere she'll be able to live. I can see her cooking in the kitchen. My kids will eventually warm up to her.

I debate on how to celebrate. Then, I decide to pick the kids up and take them to see the lodge. Since nobody is living in it, I can take them to look around the grounds. We won't be able to get inside yet. It'll still be fun for them. I call the wife. "Yeah, it's me. I was wondering if I could take the kids out today?" Unfortunately, Randy went camping with some friends. He's not home. She said Maggie and Joey are home, and they can come. I told her I'd be there in about an hour to pick them up.

On my way there, I decide to stop at Subway and pick up some hoagies to take. We could have a picnic there. I have a cover in the car still, from the last time Maggie was chilly. I stop at a corner convenience store and pick up a 6-pack of Coke. Great, this should do it!

The kids come running toward me. "Daddy, Daddy."

"You guys ready to see the new cabin?"

Joey says, "I am. That's for sure!"

Maggie chimes in, "Me too, me too!"

Joey pulls Maggie away from the front door, "I called front seat."

I say, "Don't pull on your sister's arm, Joey. You know better."

He pouts, "But I called front seat first."

"Maggie, let your brother have the front seat. You can sit in front on the way back to your mom's house."

"Ahhh, Dad. We're not spending the night?"

"Joey, you know it's a school night. I'll have you next weekend, though. By then, we can start moving stuff in. How's that sound?"

Maggie says, "Yaaaaay!"

The ride there was mostly singing, and the two children bickering back and forth about picking bedrooms out at the lodge. Personally, I think each kid will enjoy their rooms, regardless of who gets which one. They're all decent sizes and have scenic views.

"We're here, kids."

Maggie is the first one to speak up, "Oh wow, Dad! This is huge."

Joey says, "You're right, Mag. I didn't think it would be this big."

"Well, it's hard to find a smaller cabin when you kids need your own rooms. You're older now. Squashing you into sharing rooms would be one argument after the next." As I think about them squabbling, just the thought of it makes me cringe.

Joey jumps out of the car and opens Maggie's door, "Us argue, Dad? I don't know what you're talking about."

I just smile, as I put the keys in my pocket. All three of us go on the porch and peek into the windows. Joey asks, "Do we get to keep the porch swing?"

I answer, "The contract stated everything that's here, stays."

Maggie takes a seat on it. "I love it here already."

Chapter 55

Wednesday came super-fast. I'm getting ready to meet the inspector at the lodge. I'm almost there. I'm worried about where Marge is... and still no word about Alicia. It's just too coincidental if you ask me! I did try calling the police department to find out more information, but all he could say was he wasn't allowed to give me any details about the case. So, I'm in the dark.

I pull into the driveway and notice the inspector's truck is already there. I don't see him, though. I get out and walk around to the back. He's bent down, looking at the foundation. "How's it looking so far?"

He says, "The outside is in remarkable condition considering it's out here in the middle of nowhere. Whoever owned it, babied it." He stands up, wipes his hand on his pants, and holds it out. "My name's Chuck."

"I remember, we talked on the phone. I'm Cassie." I shake his hand. "I'll unlock the house."

"If you could open the back door, it would be great." He turns on the outside spigot and washes his hands.

He spends a couple of hours going through the house. I feel like I'm going crazy by the time he's done. There just wasn't anything for me to do. At one point, I imagined what it would be like to live here with Jeremy and to cook in the kitchen with him, to sleep in the bedrooms, and to relax in the living room. I mean, it doesn't really compare to the one we had built, scenery wise, but the lodge is as nice, if not nicer, on the inside.

"It passes inspection, little lady. It just needs a few minor repairs." He hands me a copy of the paper, going over the details he paid attention to that I must have overlooked.

I call Albert, all excited. "It passed inspection!!!"

"It did?! That's great news, Cassie." He gets quiet for a moment, then continues, "Does this mean I can move in faster?"

"I'll get in contact with the owners and see about signing the paperwork tomorrow. We can meet at Castle's Title Company."

He asks, "So, I can get the keys from you after?"

"You sure can." He seems in an awful big hurry to get in.

"I'll see you tomorrow then." I click end on the phone. I walk over to Chuck. I tell him, "Thanks." He's putting his tools back in his truck.

He turns around to look at me. "You're welcome. It was a pleasure doing business with you, Cassie. I'm sure we'll see each other more often if you're working with Danica now."

"Oh, it's just temporary." I don't really feel like explaining Marge's disappearance to Chuck. He doesn't know her, and the whole situation will make me cry right now.

As I'm driving home, I call Jeremy. "Hey, babe! Do you need me to pick up something to eat or???"

He says, "I have it covered. I'm making my famous pasta salad."

"That sounds delicious. Well, I'm on my way home now."

When I pull into the driveway, I can hear my boys already barking for me. They put a smile on my face, as I walk in the door. Each greeting me with their happily wagging tails. "I love you too." I pat each on the head. "Do you want to go outside? Come on, boys." They get to the back door and wait for me to throw them their treats.

I make my way back to Jeremy. "It sure smells good in here." I rub my stomach.

"I hope so... I've been working on this for the past hour."

I smile at him, "An hour isn't so bad."

"Ouch. Slave me, then cut me down." We both laugh.

He holds out a fork with noodles spun around it, toward my mouth. "Taste."

I wrap my lips around it and tell him, "Yum. It's delicious."

He winks at me and asks, "Can you set the table, baby?"

"Sure." I open a cabinet, taking out a couple of wine glasses. I grab some plates and put them by the stove. Then, I grab napkins and some eating utensils. "Ready when you are."

We have a pretty quiet dinner until he starts asking questions about Albert. I feel as grumpy as he does. It must be the guilt of kissing Albert.

He asks, "Why are you being so defensive about it? I just wanted to know if it went well."

"I'm sorry. I guess I'm just tired."

The rest of the night went smooth, which I'm thankful for because it's been a long day!

Chapter 56

Today, I meet with Albert at Castle's Title Company. I'm not looking forward to it because every time I spend time with Jeremy, the guilt of kissing Albert overwhelms me. It makes it complicated to be with him. I don't understand the want, I just know it's seriously wrong. I love Al.. shit Jeremy. I love Jeremy! What's wrong with me? I tell myself I was caught up in the moment. Nothing more, nothing less. I give Jeremy a kiss and quickly head out the door.

By the time I get to him, I'm in real estate broker mode. "Hi, Albert. It's good to see you again."

He looks at me with a stare that looks a little confused, "Cassie."

I tell him, "If you follow me to the back there's a meeting room the others are waiting for us in."

"Others?"

"Yes, the sellers, and Cheri who works with the title company. Also, my temporary partner, Danica."

He says, "Oh, okay."

When we walk into the room, we are immediately greeted. I look over at Albert, who is smiling ear to ear. I look over at the sellers as well, who are smiling just as big. This is the part I love about my job, making everyone happy. Cheri passes out the papers, they each sign.

When all is said and done, I'm relieved to be finished with Albert and the estate. "Well, Cassie, I guess this is it. I am now a proud owner of the lodge."

I respond, "Yes, you are."

He says, "Celebrate with me. Let's go for coffee or a wine."

"I can't. I still have a few more phone calls to make."

"Come on, Cassie. You have all day to make those phone calls. I just made a great offer. I want you to go with me. Otherwise, I have to celebrate alone. You don't want that, do you?"

By now, I'm feeling guilty because I did just make an abundance of money on the sale. "Okay, but only for one."

"How about we just take my car?" When he says that, I look at him with unease.

"I'm not sure that's a good idea."

"Cassie, you're being so stubborn." He opens his car door, and I get in.

He takes us further than I expected, to a town over, where there is a Bar & Grill. "I think you'll like it here, and if you're hungry, they have the best roast beef."

I do have an empty stomach and drinking on it is probably not the best idea. Yet, I don't have an appetite. "I'm not hungry." I think about Jeremy's pasta salad.

He orders us two glasses of wine. He brings mine over. I say, "Thank you." I take a drink.

A little while later, I start to feel hot and woozy. "I'm not feeling well, I think we should leave." I go to stand up and almost fall. He takes me by the arm and leads me out. He then unlocks the car and helps me in.

I wake up a few times on the drive, but I'm so tired that I fall back to sleep. All goes dark, by the time I wake up, I'm at the title company. I'm inside my car, and he's nowhere around. I feel sexually tampered with.

I look at my watch and see I have time to get home before Jeremy is there. After kissing Albert, I can't tell Jeremy about how I'm feeling. Did I ask for this? I feel so confused.

I go in and head straight to the shower. I don't even pet the dogs. I feel so dirty. After I get dressed, I make myself a cup of coffee. "You boys want to go outside?" I open the door and let them run. Shortly after, Jeremy gets home.

He asks me, "How was your day?"

I sigh, as I put myself in his arms, "It was okay." My voice becomes hoarse, "I made a sale."

He rubs my back, "Congratulations, honey! I'm so proud of you."

What did I do to deserve him? He's everything I've ever wanted in a man. He makes me laugh, and he's always here for me when I need a hug, kiss, or even a smile. I release him to his own tasks, and I make my way to the couch. I basically slam myself down, as if to punish myself. It does cause some pain. Pain I shouldn't be feeling right now, that's stronger than it was earlier. Damn that Albert. I hate him. I imagine a few scenarios of his death. Wishful thinking. At least, I'm done with him now.

"What are you watching?" Jeremy cuts off my thoughts. He tilts his head, "Looks pretty interesting."

I tune in. "Sorry, was kind of zoned, not watching or thinking about anything." The guilt overwhelms me again.

He sits on the couch next to me and wraps his arm around my shoulders. "I missed you today."

I look to the floor, "I missed you too."

Chapter 57

I whistle my way back to the apartment. What a day! Cassie's body was everything I expected it to be. She's superb. Everything I ever wanted in my woman, which she will soon be! My good mood takes me to the phone, to call the kids. When Randy answers, I have him put it on speaker, so the other two kids can hear me. "We have the keys to the lodge." The kids are as excited about it as I am. When I'm off the phone, I grab some boxes from the storage in the hall.

I decide to take care of Jeremy before I get the kids for the weekend. I must conspire a good plan of action beforehand. I spend the day packing up the kitchen. I'm going to the lodge tonight, to think of the grand scheme of things. I can map everything out and decide my actions then.

I carry the boxes to my vehicle. Once I'm on my way there, I feel relieved. There's something about being in nature that does that to me. It could have something to do with knowing Jeremy will soon be out of mine and Cassie's way. He's been a huge burden to me. I can't stand him. Why Cassie was with him in the first place, is beyond me!

When I get to the lodge, I unpack the boxes, then make my way to the basement. It's just one big room. It has one old metal, padded chair in it. I lift it and see if it's heavy. This can be used. I put it to the middle of the floor. He could scoot around on it, though. That would make a lot of noise! I don't want that. I look around the basement some more, trying to find something I can hold him to. I see pipes along the wall, but he could easily pull them apart with little strength. That's when I see a beam coming from the ceiling to the floor, toward the corner of the room. There's no plumbing or windows around it. I go over and try to shake it with no give whatsoever. Great! This will work.

I decide to go to the supply store. I can get everything I will need to hold Jeremy captive, while I get some answers from him. They pretty much had everything I needed. I throw the bags in and drive off like a bat out of hell. I'm in a hurry. It's not like I have all week. By the time I get back to the apartment, it's pitch-black outside. I decide a good night's rest will do me good. Maybe while I lie there, I'll think of something more. I look out toward Cassie's real estate agency. Well, it's not hers, but when she becomes mine, it will be.

The next day goes pretty smooth. I was unable get to Jeremy, as I had planned. He'll just have to wait until I take my kids back home. I couldn't think up a strategy fast enough for him. What a despicable man he is.

When I get the kids back to the lodge, they have boxes of stuff with them. I say, "You do realize you're not moving in, right? Though, I'd love to have you."

Maggie laughs and says, "We want some personal things in our bedrooms, Dad. Geez, we wouldn't leave Mom all alone."

They carry in their things. While they unload, I make a few phone calls from my cellular. I decide it's safer not to have a house phone. I wouldn't want Jeremy getting a hold of it. That's the last thing I need. I'm sure the beam will keep him captive, though.

When the kids are finished, I ask them, "Do you want to go for a hike later?"

Joey gets all excited, "I do, I do, Dad!"

"Okay, but you have to help me pack these sandwiches up." I put the loaf of bread away. "And get the Kool-Aid containers out of the fridge that I picked up on the way to get you.

Joey says, "I'll grab them."

Randy tells him, "Slow down Joey, or you're going to fall."

I ask, "Randy, did you by chance bring a backpack?"

He responds, "I did."

"Do you mind if we use that to pack the Kool-Aids and lunches in?"

"Sure Dad, let me grab it."

When I wake up the next morning, I'm sore as hell. The hike went well, but the old body can't take much anymore. The kids are sleeping, so I go ahead and make them breakfast. It's just a simple bacon and eggs dish. I don't have much more groceries yet. When I drop them off at home, I'll pick up more.

Chapter 58

It's been a few days, and I'm still feeling as dirty as the devil himself. I want to tell Jeremy so badly, but I know he won't forgive me. Maybe he'll even blame me. I mean, it is my fault. I want to go to the police and scream at them, tell them to get that bastard and lock him away, and just throw away the key.

After Jeremy goes to work, I just lie in bed doing the ugly cry. I feel so violated. I tell myself, if I can just will myself to take some vitamins and have a coffee, I'd feel better. Yet, I can't move. I just lie under the covers, half peeking out. All these questions are whirling around in my mind. No answers. I hate you, Albert.

I can't let that slob stop me from living my life. I must be strong. I can do this. I get myself up, heading toward the kitchen. Jeremy must have already made the coffee and left me some. I get a cup down and pour it full. I look to the floor, as I make my way into the living room. I set my cup on the coffee table and get down on the floor with the dogs. I wrap my arms around them tightly, squeezing the hugs right out of them. "I love you, boys." They sense something is wrong because they let me love them without wiggling around too much.

I think of how awful I am. I catch a glimpse of my reflection in the china hutch, and I just stare at myself for a moment. How could you? I make my way back to the bedroom and debate just lying back down. Instead, I swallow down a few vitamins and get dressed. I stare out the window, pondering something I can do to keep my mind from thinking. Otherwise, I want to keep beating myself up over this.

I call Alicia's mom, "Hi, this is Cassie. Any news?"

She clears her throat, "Oh, hi Cassie. No news. They have been tracking the purchases made at the jewelry shop. There weren't that many, so they're taking a closer look at each one individually."

"I'm sorry." As I hang up the phone, I feel a pain go deep down from my heart to my stomach. It's an ache for sure. Everything is going wrong. My friends are missing, I've been date raped, Jeremy has basically been cheated on...

I pull on a long-sleeved sweater that's loose around the shoulder, even though it's hot outside. I find myself some cotton pants. The thought of being touched makes me nauseous. I have to get myself out of this before I see Jeremy. I think about having a talk with Rose. I call her.

"Rose, this is Cassie."

"Hi Cassie! Long time no hear."

I hesitate, wondering if it has been that long. "What are you up to today?"

"Waiting for my man to get home."

"I've yet to see your new place, since you unpacked. Mind if I come over and visit with you?"

"Sure, I'll put some fresh coffee on now. See you in a bit."

I let the dogs out, while I turn the coffee pot off and slip on my shoes. By the time I'm done, I let them back in. "You be good while I'm gone. I'll stop at the store and buy you some new toys." I pat each on the head. "Be good."

I grab my keys and head out the door. The drive there is beautiful. I start to feel my shoulders relax. It will do us good when we move. It'll be a fresh start, and I can put all of this behind me. I wish it were another state... the further from Albert, the better.

When I get to Rose's, I start debating whether I should tell her or not. I look at her house, and I look at the lake. So soothing! I knock on her door, and shortly after she answers. "Get in here, girl. It's so good to see you."

I give her a hug and don't want to let go. I instantly start crying. She asks, "What's the matter, sugar?" She leads me to the couch.

I breathe in and breathe out. "You probably won't believe me if I told you."

She pats me on the back, "I sure would."

She walks into the kitchen, bringing us back a coffee. She hands me mine, and as she does, I tell her about how I sold a house to Albert. How when Jeremy had amnesia, I kissed Albert and realized what a mistake it was. I told her about selling him the lodge and how I was date raped. I let it all come pouring out of me.

She stands up, "Well, that low life scum bag! I ought to... "

"Rose, no. I just want to put it all behind me. I just needed someone to confide in."

"You need a cop and a doctor."

"No, Rose. I want to keep it between us. If Jeremy were to find out, he'd leave me. I'm not going to let Albert take him from me too."

Rose is murmuring bad things about Albert, as she paces back and forth. "What I could do to that monster."

I change the subject, "Your place looks great."

She takes the hint and grabs my hand. "Did I show you the new dining room table?"

It's one of Rose's best qualities. She's a good listener and not judgmental. She also knows how to leave well enough alone. I don't feel like crying or talking about it anymore, and it's as if she just gets it. She guides me into the dining room.

She says, "Here it is... ta-da."

It's antique white and painted to look old. "I love it, Rose, I really do."

As I drive home, I realize just how valuable my time with

Rose was. I feel so much better now. It's getting dark. I stop at the pet shop and pick up some chew bones and toys for the dogs. Just as I had promised them I would. I also make a stop at the local grocer for some wine. I'm going to need it to sleep the whole night through. Otherwise, I'll just be awake thinking it all over one too many times.

Chapter 59

It's been over a week since Albert made my life a living hell. Things are starting to settle down with me. Out of sight and out of mind. I've been concentrating more on Jeremy. Since the office isn't open, I've been home more, which has been good for me. I've been packing box after box. The only room left to do is the bedroom. I've procrastinated that because it's our clothes and where we sleep. The master bath needs packed too.

"Jeremy! Should we start packing the bedroom now?"

He pokes his head around the door from the hallway. "Yeah, I say let's pack it and bring the boxes to the cabin. We'll spend the night there."

"Our bed's not there."

"Come on, sweetie. We can make a pallet on the floor." He wraps his arms around me. "I think it'll be romantic."

A night at the cabin with Jeremy does sound good. "Okay." I go into the master bath closet and pull out some blankets. "But I'm taking my pillow."

He laughs and says, "You and me both." He plays with a few strands of my hair, "How about we leave early today and go for a hike around the lake?"

"Sounds like a plan to me!"

A few hours later, and that's just what we're doing. There are houses along the trail, but they look very cozy. It's quite the view. Jeremy says, "I thought tomorrow morning I'd go get us some donuts and milk. I thought we could eat on the dam."

"Wow, you're really going out of your way in the romance department."

"You deserve it, babe. You've really worked hard this year." As he says it, I can feel my heart drop. I'm covered in guilt.

The rest of the night we lie on the floor talking for hours. I guess we finally fell asleep around one in the morning.

By the time I wake up, Jeremy is back with donuts. I ask, "Where'd you get those?"

"There's a gas station off 72. They get fresh donuts daily. They even brag about it." His smile broadens. He lifts the half gallon of milk. "We will have to share. They didn't have any cups or glasses."

I smile at him, "But what if I get your cooties."

He answers, "Babe, I hate to break it to you... but you already have them." We both laugh.

We make our way down our gravel hill, to the road... down the grassy hill to the dam. We both take a seat on the ground, and he opens the box of donuts. I say, "Yum, custard."

"The finest for my darling." He hands it to me.

We spend about an hour eating, drinking milk, and talking about our future plans. He wants us to start thinking about having a baby right away. I tell him, "I think it's wise if we marry first."

He finally agrees, at the end. I told him I'd feel fat in a wedding gown if I was pregnant. He said we wouldn't wait that long to get married. I still told him I'd rather wait, and he patiently agreed on my terms.

He says, "Let's go fishing!"

"We don't have any gear. Besides, don't you have to work?"

"Oh honey, I'm my own boss. I'm taking the day off. Come on, let's walk back. We'll hit the Outdoors Sporting Goods store. It's only ten minutes away."

I debate going. I've turned into somewhat of a recluse

since Albert date raped me. "Okay, it kind of sounds like fun."

He asks, "Going to the store or going fishing?"

I pinch him, "Both."

We get everything we need at the store, and on the drive home I seriously look him over. He asks, "What's gotten into you lately? It's like you've never seen me."

"Geez babe, you did have amnesia. It was like I didn't see you. I just... I missed you."

He smiles, and we both start singing to the song playing on the radio.

When we get home, he unloads the bags onto the picnic table that's on our front porch. I sit on the porch swing and watch him fix the line on the fishing pole. He hands it to me, "This one is yours." Then he starts on his. I watch him put the bait on.

"Are you ready?" He asks me, as he starts down the hill.

"Well, wait up. My legs are tired from this morning. This is the most exercise I've had all year."

He stops and turns around, holding out his hand that I take in mine. I smile really big, knowing he's all mine. He says, "We'll go to the grassy island. Sound like a plan to you?"

I respond, "Yep," as I follow him.

He has me cast out first then he does it. We stand there for a while, and before we know it, I have a snag. "I think I have a fish, honey."

He excitedly says, "Reel it in!!!"

It turned out to be a small blue gill. We throw it back in. However, the intensity of it left me wanting to catch an even bigger one.

Dusk is hitting. No luck on any fish fry, that's for sure. We had fun just the same. Jeremy said next time we're fishing at one of the lakes at the top of the hill across from us. He says, "Tomorrow I'm going back to our house and collecting some more boxes. I want you to sleep in."

Chapter 60

Jeremy is at their house I looked in to buying. I get behind Jeremy and do a chokehold on him. He's a thin guy, so it made it easy for me. He didn't see me coming, sucker. I don't strangle him to death because I need information from him. I just do it long enough to where he passes out. I throw him in the front seat of his vehicle, so I can keep an eye on him. I search his jean pockets and sure enough there's the keys.

When I get to the lodge, I have to drag him by his arms down the stairs. I'm sure his legs are bruised, hitting each step as we go. I guess that's better. There's less chance of an escape if he's hurt. I take him to the corner. I handcuff him to the beam. He can't get loose. I go back upstairs before he can come out of his coma-like state. I don't feel like the drama that comes with him discovering that he's been captured. I decide to give him until tomorrow. I could use the sleep anyway.

The next morning, I go downstairs with water. He's not appreciative whatsoever. In fact, not only does he spit it out, but he spits it all over me. I say, "It's okay, I don't like you either. The only reason you're still alive is because I have questions for you."

I can tell he's not in any mood to cooperate with me, so I go back upstairs. I make myself some breakfast. I let him scream it out for a few hours before he realizes nobody can hear him. He's getting on my nerves, so I go outside to chop some wood.

Jackie Adams

A few hours pass, and when I go inside, it's finally quiet. I fill another glass with water and take it downstairs. "After all that screaming, I'm sure you're thirsty. You've probably discovered by now that nobody can hear you." I hold the glass up to his mouth, and he gulps it down.

Jeremy looks confused and asks, "Why am I here? Who are you? What do you want with me?"

I take the glass of water, set it on the step, and walk back over, "You're here because I want to know more about Cassie."

He slides his handcuffs up the beam and stands, "I'm not telling you a damn thing about Cassie. What's your business with her?"

I answer, "It's quite simple, really. She belongs with me. She's my soulmate."

He starts kicking his leg out toward me, "She's mine. I'm going to marry her."

I walk over to him and punch him in his face, "No, you're always in the way. She's not a piece of property to be owned. She's already been with me. She just does it behind your back."

His nose is bleeding. "You lying piece of shit."

I chokehold him again, and he struggles into a slumber. He's not going to give me the answers I need. Should I try one more time or just kill him?! As I debate to myself, I hear sirens. What the hell?!

I go upstairs, and there's two police at my door. The policeman standing closest to me asks, "Are you Albert Wilson?" He holds out his badge.

"I am." I come out onto the porch and shut the door. "We're wondering if you've seen this woman?" The second policeman holds out a photograph of Alicia.

"She looks vaguely familiar." I take the photo in my hand and study it a little harder. "I can't place her."

Jeremy must have woken up and heard us talking because he starts screaming. A cop pushes past me and enters the lodge. I follow him, while the other officer is behind me. I turn quickly and grab his pistol and shoot the other cop dead. Then, I turn on the other officer and shoot him. Great, just great. This is the last thing I needed, two dead officers.

I go down to the basement, in frustration. "Do you know what you just made me do? Kill two innocent policemen. This is all your fault." I punch him in his face again. "You scream one more time and the next death will be yours."

I go back upstairs, drag the bodies out, and put them inside the cop car. I drive to my lake and dispose of the car in it. I hate doing this because the lake is on my property. I know it's stupid, but it's a quick fix. I'm not sure what else to do right now.

I drive his car to the next town over and park it at a Walmart. Then I go to a bar and call a Uber to give me a ride down the street from their house. I walk the rest of the way and get in my vehicle.

I wonder if Cassie is home.

Chapter 61

I'm a nervous wreck. Jeremy didn't come home all night. I haven't had a wink of sleep, and when I went to file a missing person's report, I didn't feel like the police took me seriously enough. I know he told me he was going to our other house to load some boxes. I spent the night there. The police, they made it sound like he didn't want to come home or was having an affair. I try calling Jeremy's cell phone again. This time it doesn't ring. It goes straight to voicemail, like it does when it has lost its charge.

I'm pacing the floor and biting my nails. "Where are you, Jeremy?" I decide to go for a drive to our new house. Maybe he's there. Maybe somehow, he got caught up in work and got there late. I guess I was going faster than I realized because a cop pulls in behind me with his sirens on. I get my driver's license and insurance card ready.

He comes to my window, "You do realize how fast you were going, right?"

"I'm sorry officer, I didn't. I just finished filing a missing person's complaint, and I was going to look for my fiancé at his work location. I'm a nervous reck."

"Then maybe you should be at home, at least until you start feeling calmer. You can't go breaking the laws." He takes my driver's license and insurance card back to his car. I must have sat there twenty minutes before he comes back to my window. He says, "Make sure you slow down." When he hands me the ticket, I notice how badly my hand is shaking.

"Yes, sir."

I continue my journey to the new house. I bite my lip, he could be having an affair? Or is that my conscience from the bad choices I've made. When I get in the gate, I drive to his work location, and there's no sign of his vehicle. I drive around the valley and the top of the hills. I get to our place and there's no vehicle. I get out and go sit on the porch swing, staring out at the lake. I try to think of where else he might be. I think back to any places he told me he might stop. I got nothing.

I get on my cell phone that has crappy signal, but still dials through. "Rose?"

"Yeah?"

"Jeremy didn't come home all night. I filed a missing person's report. I don't think they're taking this seriously, though."

She asks, "Did you try calling him?"

I respond, "Numerous times. So much now that I'm assuming he's lost charge on his phone. Oh Rose, I have a bad feeling."

"Do you want me to come over?"

"Yeah, sure... just give me a bit to get home. I'm closer to your house, but I don't want to stay here. I want to be home in case Jeremy comes walking in. I'm just confused to which one I should be at. I guess I'll go back to our old one where the dogs are. They need more of my attention by now." I turn my car back around.

"I have to shower and get dressed. I'll stop at the coffee shop and bring us a cup. See you in a bit."

As I click end on my phone, I feel a deep ache in my chest. It's a burning hollowness. A sense of loss, which confuses me this soon. I play my music loud enough to distract my thoughts, as I eye the speedometer. When I get home, I let the dogs out. I know Jeremy isn't here because his car isn't outside. I look for signs that he may have been, with no such luck.

I check the answering machine. Nothing. I even check caller I.D. I hear a knock. Great, Rose is here. "Come on in."

As I walk out of the kitchen into the living room, I almost faint when I see Albert standing there. "What are you doing here?" I ask, as I nervously walk to the opposite side of the room.

"I wanted you to know that we can be together now. I've missed you, Cassie."

"What do you mean by be together, Albert? I have a fiancé." I nervously push my bangs from my eyes.

"Fiancé, come on Cassie. You were just with him to pass the time. I'm ready for you now, and he's out of our way... so are Alicia and Marge. We don't have to worry about them either. I figure you can open your own real estate agency once you and I get married."

"What? You sound crazy. I don't love you, Albert. I don't want to be with you." I guess that was the wrong thing to say. He put his huge hand around my small neck and pulled me to the door.

He says, "You're coming with me, Cassie."

Chapter 62

Albert has me thrown over his shoulder. He must still think I'm sleeping. I guess the rain woke me. I don't remember any of the trip here to get to his lodge. I see the lightning flash as he carries me inside. He puts me on a recliner and walks into the kitchen. As slowly and quietly as I can, I get up and make my escape out the front door, but I decide to go back inside and hide. By the time I'm at the bottom of the lodge, he must have heard me. I go to the back and see a door. He's screaming out my name as I fumble with the knob.

The door is locked. I search for a rock. When I find one, I wait until the thunder roars, and then I break the glass so I can reach in and unlock it. Once I get in, I'm only there for a minute before I climb the stairs. It smells like there's a rotting corpse in the corner. It's too dark to see, and all I can think about is escaping. I open the upstairs door and peek inside. He must still be outside looking for me. I go inside and search for a phone, but I don't have any luck. Then, I see his cellular. I dial 911 right before I hear him coming back inside.

I quickly run down the hall and see the attic cord. I pull it down. I climb up, taking the cord inside with me as I shut the attic door. He says, "I heard you, Cassie." I can hear Albert, as he's dragging a ladder across the floor.

I whisper, "Hello? Is this 911? Can you hear me?" There is no response. I look at the signal, and there isn't one. Dammit! I hear the door creek open. I remind myself to remain calm and to stay quiet. My heart is thudding out of my chest. I swallow down hard and hold my breath.

"Cassie, I can hear you." His repulsive voice echoes throughout the empty attic. "When I find you, there won't be any need for words. You will FEEL the frustration you have caused me."

I know he means business. I had smelled what I assume is a dead body that is rotting away in the basement. The stomach-turning stench greeted me like a nightmare from hell. My only prayer is that it is not my boyfriend, Jeremy. Suddenly, I feel the back of my head explode in a million different directions.

By the time my eyes open, he's dragging me by my ponytail. My fingernails are dredging through the wet, muddy grass. I'm camouflaged in the earth's soil, and every part of my body feels like it's sinking with his long, harsh pulls. I try to reach up, but I can only move my eyes. I quickly shut them again. Maybe he'll think I'm dead. Maybe he'll just drop my body off somewhere and leave me be. It could be hopeful thinking, but that's all I have left. Please, please, I think to myself, leave me alive.

He stops and starts digging a hole. Does he think I'm already dead? I'm able to move my body now. Should I get up from here and run? Can I run? Should I stand and fight him? He's much bigger than I am. I don't think I'd stand a chance fighting him. I slowly stand up and quietly walk away, as he digs in the mud. I go back toward the house and hide behind a tree. I know there's not any sense in trying to walk to the road. There's no hope for a ride. It's vacant, especially at this time of night. Right when I was ready to lose all hope. I see flashes of light coming up the narrow road.

Oh my God, it's the cops! I run out in front of one of their vehicles, waving my arms in the air. I see one, two, three cop vehicles. The squad car stops, "Ma'am what are you doing out here?" I explain everything to her inside the vehicle, as fast as I can. I tell them where I left Albert digging the hole. I'm still in shock, so the whole, he's going to bury me bit, hasn't kicked in yet.

The policewoman gets out of her car and walks to the one behind it. I can hear her telling him what I told her. They walk in the direction of where Albert was. When they come back, I can see they've apprehended him. They put him inside the police car. Once the thunder subsides, we start hearing shouting from inside the house. "HELP!" The cops go in, and the next thing I know, they're bringing Jeremy out. I jump out of the vehicle and run toward him as fast as I can. A cop stops me and says he's injured. They call for an ambulance. His face is covered in blood. He's so weak that a cop is holding him up.

I tell the cops that Albert confessed to killing Alicia and Marge. I also told them about his stalking, and how he had a made-up scenario in his head, of the two of us being together. They ask me if I'll testify to it in court. Of course, I tell them yes, I will.

I asked them, "How did you know to come?" "Because we knew two of our cops were coming out here, and we hadn't heard from them for quite a while, so we came out." The cops put Jeremy and me in their car, and took us home.

The rest was something I don't want to remember. It was all a blur. Jeremy recovered, then there was the trial. I had to testify and that was not fun. Anyway, Albert was convicted, and now he's behind bars, I hope forever.

Chapter 63

I hear the baby crying. "It's your turn, Mrs. Jeremiah Banks."

I toss and turn on the bed, "But Jeremy, I thought I did it last time." My eyes are so heavy. I'm full of exhaustion.

"It's only fair you have your turn now." He pulls and tugs at me.

"Okay, okay. I'll get our precious vocal cords out of bed and hold her." I sit up, rubbing my eyes. I have no doubt they're blood shot red.

I walk into the nursery. It's across the hall from our bedroom. It's large enough to have a changing table and a rocking chair beside the cradle. I pick up Maggie May and say, "I love you, precious." I give her a kiss on her forehead. Then, I sit on the rocking chair next to the window and rock her.

Jeremy brings in a bottle. "Here you go. I thought she might be hungry."

I laugh, "You mean, there are times she's NOT hungry?"

"You're right. She loves her milk."

Jeremy goes back to bed, and I sing to Maggie, as she eats.

I'm glad to know that Albert is serving his time. He confessed to the deaths of Alicia and Marge and the two policemen. He also confessed to kidnapping Jeremy and stalking me. I never said a word about the kiss or date rape. It's something I have to live with daily, but if it means not losing Jeremy, then it's something I'm willing to do.

I pull Maggie May up and lean her against my shoulder.

I'm going to burp her. I start singing our song, "You are my sunshine..." Once she's finally asleep, I put her in her crib and go back into the bedroom with Jeremy.

"I really miss Alicia and Marge," I wipe a tear away.

Jeremy turns to his side, facing me, "I know you do, honey."

We live in our dream house, we're married, and now we have a daughter. Jeremy wants more children. If we do, I'm going to name them after Alicia and Marge... or would that be too much of a constant reminder?! I blame myself for their disappearance. Albert kept saying they were in the way.

"Jeremy, are you still awake?"

"Yeah, baby. What's up?"

"Their deaths are my fault." I wipe away another tear.

"Their deaths are not your fault. Albert is a lunatic. He's an unbelievably bad man. He enjoys hurting other people. If not you, he would have focused on somebody else. Stop being so hard on yourself."

I snuggle in his arms and rest my head on his chest. He holds me tightly. He says, "Remember, nights are always more emotional. You'll always miss them, but tomorrow you'll feel stronger when you're not so physically and mentally drained."

"You're right. I need to stop blaming myself. Thanks for listening to me, honey." Soon after, I fall asleep in his arms, knowing he's right... the next day will be a little easier.

Jackie Adams is an emerging author who lives in Missouri with her teenage son and her two dogs.

www.ingramcontent.com/pod-product-compliance
Lightning Source LLC
Chambersburg PA
CBHW030748190726
48285CB00003B/759